The Pink Ribbon

A Tale of Romance, Tragedy, and Triumph

A novel by

Alice Louise

Mind's Eye Media, LLC
Grove City, Ohio

ISBN-10: 0692446559
ISBN-13: 978-0692446553

PRINTED IN THE UNITED STATES OF AMERICA

Published by Mind's Eye Media, LLC
Grove City, Ohio
mindseyecols@yahoo.com

Dedication

THIS BOOK is dedicated to my dear daughter and cheerleader, RaMarie, who donated hours of time and energy preparing this book for publication. Thank you.

Contents

Prologue

MARIA GALLIO hated the rough passage across the Atlantic by sailing ship. She would have rather stayed in Italy, but her husband Anthony was adamant about the migration of his small family to America. He hoped for a better life for Maria and their two-year-old daughter Teresa. The United States of America held his dreams for his family, he thought. The year was 1848.

Settling in Franklinton, center of a coal mining industry that dotted the Allegheny Mountains, Anthony became a miner in the Glenn coal mines.

The riches envisioned by Gallio were hard won, if to be realized at all. With his meager wages and Maria's help, he managed to keep bread on the table. Maria, in turn, did laundry for several of the more prominent families in town.

In 1850, Matthew Gallio was born, a lusty ten-pound baby with enormous dark eyes. His parents were proud that the child could claim full citizenship in their adopted country.

Ten years saw little change in the lifestyle of Maria and Anthony. Eighteen-sixty was not a good year for the family.

On a cold March day, the alarm whistle at the Glenn mine blew its rapid, staccato warning out over the town. "Cave in. Cave in!" People started screaming.

Maria, busy scrubbing clothes for the town doctor, dropped what she was doing to run toward the mine. "Oh God in heaven," Maria prayed, "not my Anthony."

Rain was drenching the town as Maria dragged herself the quarter mile up the hill clutching her wet skirts that were tangled around her ankles. She pushed through the throng of people approaching the gaping, black entrance to the mine. Men were corralling everyone, telling them to keep back. A rope was strung across the opening to act as a barrier. The desperate families wept and screamed, waiting to hear some word about their loved ones.

"Let me by...oh, Mary Mother of Jesus, let me by, my Anthony might be down there!" No one moved. Their faces were twisted with fear and grief. They stood like a stone wall.

Ten-year-old Matthew held his sister's hand as they joined their mother at the mine site. "Mama, Mama, is Pa down in the cave in?" the boy questioned.

"I don't know...I don't know." She wept. Teresa, soaked through, tried to comfort her mother by patting her hand. "Pa ain't down there, is he?" She pleaded with her eyes.

Two hours passed before the mine manager posted the names of the trapped men on the pay shack wall. Anthony Gallio's name was third on the list. Hope for the buried men diminished with each hour. The action around the coal mine was feverish all night. Rain pelted the crowd, adding to the misery of the victims' families. Miners rode the rails. Carload after carload of men were pulled by mules into the dark cavity of the mine.

Although only a child, Matthew knew he would never forget those brave men, their faces black with coal dust, their muscled arms with corded veins standing out as they clutched the picks and shovels, looking with determined faces toward what lay below in the dark pit. Some of them spit tobacco juice as if to express their disdain for the tragedy they were all a part of. Others were cursing to cover up their grievous frustration. All of them were suffering the hell that comes only with a mine cave-in. Those faces were etched in Matthew's memory forever.

At dawn, Teresa asked her brother to help her. "Matthew, lift Ma up." They both pulled a soaked, freezing Maria to her feet. The two children half carried, half dragged their mother back to the shack they called home.

The rescue team worked for three days to reach the buried men. They were all dead, twenty of them.

After they buried Anthony, nothing was the same for the Gallios. Teresa, watching her mother's health deteriorate, quit school. She was fourteen and old enough to take a job as a maid for the mine owner's wife. Agatha Glenn had two lively children. Teresa found a place for herself at the Glenns that enabled her to bring home much needed money.

Maria tried to carry on as a laundress but was often ill. The light seemed to go out of her dark eyes after her husband's death.

Father Timothy Cassidy, the Parrish priest, visited the Gallios often. He was troubled by Maria's weakening condition. Teresa, by then barely fifteen, could not keep the small family together for long. Matthew would be the one to suffer most if anything happened to his mother; that's what Father Cassidy thought. A foreboding hung over the old priest's head about the Gallios. God willing, nothing would come of it.

The Glenn house was a large, white clapboard edifice with fifteen rooms. Agatha Glenn had designed it herself. The square tower that rose on the side of the house held her retreat at the top, away from the hustle and bustle of the family.

The tower room was where she did her reading, sewing, and thinking. It had wide windows in the rear overlooking the green majesty of the mountain ridge known as Bear Mountain, an extensive ridge that lined the deep valley in which Franklinton was built.

Teresa was proud of her position in the Glenn household, if only a maid; they treated her like family. She blossomed during the two years she was employed there.

Three days after her sixteenth birthday, she went to her mother. "I've met a young man, Ma. He has a good job at Elroy's lumber mill. His name is Jim Bird."

Maria's illness had worsened. She just coughed helplessly and looked at her daughter with empty eyes. Teresa went on, "He takes me to church on

Sundays, in the lumber yard wagon. Mr. Elroy says he has a real future there."

Maria only patted Teresa's hand softly.

Matthew, too, was busy trying to help with the household expenses. He was employed by Bean's grocery store to deliver groceries after school.

On March 14, 1862, he finished his last delivery of the day and was hurrying home in a heavy downpour of rain. Entering the shack, he found Maria on her back on the floor in front of the woodstove where water was boiling furiously. Coffee lay spilled on the floor. Her dark dress was tangled around her ankles and she clutched a corner of her apron in one hand. Her black eyes stared sightlessly at the ceiling.

Sobbing and choking, Matthew ran out into the rain toward the Catholic church and Father Cassidy. The old Priest heard his pounding. He opened the door and young Matthew fell into his arms. "You gotta come quick...Ma's awful sick. Come quick, Father, please. I don't know what to do, and Teresa ain't home yet."

"Slow down now, son, I'm moving as fast as I can."

He drew on his overcoat, picked up his umbrella, and took the boy's hand in his. The two sloshed through the mud, running toward the Gallio shack.

Father Cassidy administered last rites to Maria Gallio, exactly two years to the day after Anthony Gallio's death.

The two children were grief stricken. Teresa tried to keep house for Matthew, continuing her work at the Glenn's. There were days when she felt unable to continue being mother to Matthew and maid at the mine owner's house. If it weren't for Father Cassidy's counsel she might have given up.

Six months after Maria's passing, Teresa stood at the priest's door, her face wan and unsure of herself. Father Cassidy's housekeeper, Julia Keep, answered her first knock. "I came to talk to the Father about a decision I must make."

The priest heard her arrival. "Come in to my study, child, and sit over here by my desk." He motioned her toward a large side-chair by the old, scarred desk. Seeing her pulling nervously on her bonnet ribbons, he tried to put her at ease. "And how are things going for you and your brother?"

"That's what I must talk to you about. I have no one else to turn to."

"I've always left my door open to you, Teresa. You know that. Whatever you need, I'll do my best."

"I may need more than you can give, Father."

"Let me be the judge of that."

"I've been seeing a young man. His name is Jim Bird. He works at Elroy's lumber yard. Well...he has high hopes for the future...."

The old man punched tobacco into his pipe bowl. Hm...Ummm," he nodded his bald head, his blue eyes concerned, his pink face turned toward her with encouragement, listening.

Teresa went on, "Jim's been offered a better job at his uncle's lumber mill in Pittsburgh and...well, he asked me to marry him and go along." The girl lowered her head and picked at the drawstring on her small reticule.

"Well, Teresa, does that make you happy?"

"Oh yes, Father, it makes me very happy but..."

"But what?"

"It's a wonderful opportunity for both of us, except, we won't be making much money to start with. I'm not sure what to do about Matthew. I can't take him along...least, not for a while. We ain't gonna be able to afford another mouth to feed."

Crying and desperate, Teresa told the priest that if she passed up this chance for a life, she might not get another chance. "But, if I can't make arrangements for Matthew, I won't."

Father Cassidy sat silent for a few moments. "Would you consider leaving the boy in my charge until such a time as you and your husband would be able to take him back?"

"Oh Father!" Teresa dropped to her knees in front of the priest. "Would you do that?"

"I would do that," he said as he leaned over pulling her hands up, helping her to get off her knees.

"That way he could stay in school and keep his job! I wouldn't be worrying all the time about him."

"Matthew will be fine." Father Cassidy assured her.

"You'll make him do chores, won't you? And, Father, Ma always said that he had magic in his hands. She meant because of his drawing. He draws real good. Maybe you could get him to keep drawing his pictures. It seems to make him happy and keeps him out of harm's way."

The agreement was struck.

Chapter 1: Transcendence

AGATHA GLENN sat in the tower room, surveying her small kingdom of Franklinton. She smiled to herself at the thought of being a ruler. "Ludicrous," she murmured to herself. This was her haven...this room away from the chaos of her two young, noisy children, and the constant planning for meals and overseeing the help.

The Glenn house, large and elegant, its white siding newly painted, seemed to shimmer in the afternoon sunshine, one turret pointing toward the clouds.

Never tiring of the view, she leaned on one of the window sills looking out. The quaint bench-lined square in the middle of the town was in the front, and the view of Bear Mountain in the rear gave Agatha an insight into the comings and goings of the townspeople few others could enjoy. And she did enjoy it as often as she could.

The pristine brick courthouse built in 1830 stood on one side of the square. On the opposite side, St. Joseph's Catholic Church stolidly stood sentinel. The First Methodist Church, where the Glenns attended church, occupied the fourth corner.

Not a gossip, Agatha nevertheless had a healthy curiosity about the people of her town. No one had any idea how much information she held to herself about the place and its people.

Since her husband, Conrad Glenn, employed about fifty percent of the men who lived in Franklinton in his coal mines, Agatha looked upon herself as a sort of civic protector. She had even felt some responsibility for the miners' families since she married Glenn eighteen years before in Pittsburgh. She fit into place as social leader, trendsetter, and philanthropist in the small town.

It was two o'clock in the afternoon when Father Cassidy rushed out of St. Joseph's rectory, his coat tails flying, his black hat askew in the March wind. He hurried across the square, looking neither to the right nor to the left, his feet speeding toward the schoolhouse behind Glenn House. A few minutes later, he emerged with young Matthew Gallio, age twelve, by his side. The two, the boy and the old priest, retraced Father Cassidy's footsteps back to the rectory.

Agatha watched, a thoughtful frown on her long, rigid face. What could have possibly been important enough to cause the priest to take his young ward, Matthew, out of his classes at school?

Inside the rectory, Father Cassidy led the boy into his study. He sat down behind his well-worn desk, his pink face beaming.

"Come! Sit down, Matthew! You've done it! You've won the Alistair French award for the best painting in the junior division." Matthew's dark eyes became huge, his breathing heavy; he was having trouble catching his breath he was so excited.

"I really won?"

"Yes, son, you really won. Look. Look, here's the letter." The old man waved the paper under the boy's nose. "Here, you read it."

Matthew carefully grasped the sides of the expensive vellum paper.

"Read it!...Read it out loud."

Matthew began:

The jury for the fifth annual Artists League Art Competition for the city of Philadelphia is happy to award the Alistair French Award of Merit in the junior division to Matthew Gallio of Franklinton, Pennsylvania. First place is for your painting, A Mountain Pond.

We hope that you will continue to grow in your artistic endeavors and receive further honors.

Sincerely,
James French, Administrator and Art League President

There was a note attached from Mr. French. Matthew, read that aloud:

Along with the prize money of $75.00, we are pleased to inform you that, according to the application agreement, your painting went on *sale and was purchased by Mrs. Clarinda Bartholomew for the generous amount of $50.00. Please find two separate checks enclosed.*

Signed, J. French, February 20, 1853.

The study door opened with a squeak. Julia Keep, the house-keeper for the rectory, stood looking at the two, her face a study in curiosity. "What's all the fuss about around here?"

"Come in, Julia. Matthew has done us all proud. He's won the French award for painting!"

Crossing herself, Julia walked across the room and placed her work-worn hands on the boy's shoulders. She was a wraith of a woman. Tall, too thin, and her skin looked as if it never felt the sun. Her demeanor was solid and just. A fair, good woman who was devoted to the church and her friends.

Looking squarely into Matthew's eyes, she reminded him of the times she had assured him that if he persevered and prayed, he would succeed. "This calls for a celebration." she suggested.

"How about a beef pot roast for dinner and chocolate cake?"

The priest and the boy both nodded enthusiastically.

When the housekeeper was gone, Father Cassidy asked, "Do you know what this can mean for you, son? This means you can go to Philadelphia this summer and study with Arthur Cowan, the great painter-teacher."

Instead of joy at the prospect, the boy frowned. "But, I don't want to leave here."

"It would only be for the summer. You've come a long way, young man. God gave you this gift. Don't you think the least you can do is try to make the most of it?"

"I don't want to go away to such a big place. Couldn't I just stay here and work on my painting?"

In the end, Matthew was enrolled with Arthur Cowan for the summer, junior program. The $125.00 was just enough to cover his tuition and living expenses for three months.

Chapter 2: Enlightenment

I҆T'S A SAD DAY, the boy thought, when the train to Philadelphia pulled out of the small station in Franklinton with him aboard. Father Timothy, in his black suit that was pressed so often it shined like patent leather, and Julia Keep, her long stern face slightly flushed, waved once as he boarded.

The train chugged and steamed its way down the mountain toward Philadelphia, leaving a smoky trail like an iron dragon in distress.

Matthew's arrival in the city of brotherly love was not propitious. He was met at the busy depot by a small weasel-of-a-man with a short black mustache and a goatee to match. When the man smiled, his big, yellow teeth showed. Curtly, he snapped orders to the black wagon driver he called Mose. The man spewing the orders was Reginald Yerby.

Two other boys disembarked from the same train. They, too, were new arrivals for the summer art classes. Their leather luggage was piled high in the rear of the wagon before Matthew's canvas bag was loaded onto the heap.

Mose drove the wagon with the four passengers slowly through the narrow streets lined with block after block of brick townhouses that were barely a couple of yards from the streets. He prodded the horse on past the crowds of people and peddlers until they were on the outskirts of the city. Raising dust on a curving lane, the group arrived at the Cowan estate on the northern edge of Philadelphia.

Matthew's quick view of the town only served to reinforce his feelings of regret that he had traveled to the place. The size of the city and the crowds of people frightened him. Of course, at twelve years of age he would never admit that. Tall for his age and thin, he pushed at his curly, black hair as he looked up at the Cowan edifice—a place he would spend many hours of his life.

The Cowan House was a sturdy brick building with a mansard roof and four tall chimneys, one at each corner of the house. The front entrance was framed by two Doric columns connected to a small roof designed for carriages to disembark visitors under cover.

Mose stopped the horse under the portico and the boys tumbled out.

"Here, here, young men! You'll each carry your own luggage to the small building over there." Zerby pointed to a sturdy, clapboard building close by the manor house. "That's the dormitory for students. Follow me. I'll assign you to a room. Call me MISTER Zerby."

The boys filed into a cheerful but sparsely furnished center hall off of which were eight numbered doors. "There will be two of you to a room."

Bewildered, Matthew stood mutely holding onto his bag.

The other two boys, more vocal, called out to Zerby that they'd take room number one.

"As your cottage counselor, I am in room number one. You, Terrence Bradley, and Jonathan Plummer will share room number two, if you like. Gallio, you're in room number six. You'll be sharing it with James Peabody when he arrives.

The rooms were a good size with single beds neatly made.

Two side chairs, two clothes chests, and two large-topped tables.

An over-sized window with the blind pulled halfway down gave a good light. There were no floor coverings on the wide floorboards, no drapes at the windows.

Zerby, still standing in the hall, informed the boys the bathroom was at the end of the hall, while the toilet was outside, a distance from the back door.

"You are to use the basins each one of you has in your room to wash each morning. A bath will be scheduled for you on a rotating basis each Saturday.

Matthew's stomach felt queasy. He was sweating around his collar. Would he ever get used to this place?

Zerby's weasel voice rasped on. "You may all have free time until Mr. Cowan meets with you in the main house for lunch and introductions at 12:00 o'clock noon on the dot!"

At the mention of food, Matthew bolted for the rear door, leaving Zerby with a sour expression on his face.

"My, my. Must have eaten too much, breakfast," he mused out loud, his lips curled distastefully. Under his breath... "The little WOP!"

During the two hours before their lunch meeting with Arthur Cowan, Matthew managed to pull himself together. His stomach no longer threatened to erupt. His fondest wish was to be out of Philadelphia and back home. But he knew that was not possible.

He went to the bathroom and bathed his face in cool water. A small mirror atop his dresser allowed him to survey the damage done by his sick spell. All in all, he guessed he looked normal. Taking a comb from his bag he tried to force his tight, black curls away from his face. He hated his curly hair for which he took a lot of kidding. His midnight-blue eyes were large and shined with anxiety. His generous mouth that so often smiled to show even, perfect white teeth, was tightly closed.

The three boys and Zerby waited in the parlor of the Cowan house for the teacher to appear. Matthew was very nervous.

Terrence and Jonathan lounged on a tapestry sofa while Matthew sat off in a corner on a straight-backed, side chair. Zerby stood in front of the huge marble fireplace gazing up at a large portrait of a beautiful young woman holding a small, fluffy white dog on her lap. Her blue dinner dress billowed out around her petite frame. Matthew thought she was the most beautiful lady he had ever seen.

Arthur Cowan entered the parlor. He appeared to be self-assured, pleasant of face, and a man who fit into his surroundings. Spare, barely more than five feet seven inches tall, with graying-brown, collar-length hair. His dark blue broadcloth coat and trousers were immaculate, pressed perfectly.

"Well, young men, I see you've made yourselves at home. Fine. Fine. Mr. Zerby, please introduce me to my students."

Zerby's eyes moved over the group as he pointed a bony finger at each boy. "This is Terrence Bradley, Jonathan Plummer...," then scarcely looking at Matthew, he said, "and this is uh...oh yes...Gallio!"

"Matthew Gallio?" Cowan asked.

Matthew nodded his head silently.

"Good show, young man! I saw your painting, A Mountain Pond—wasn't that the title?"

The boy nodded his head again, blushing furiously.

"Come on in to lunch, gentlemen."

Much to Matthew's surprise, Mose stood at the door to the dining room dressed in black livery. Everything seemed so formal. There wasn't any way, Matthew thought, that he'd ever fit into these surroundings.

The maid, Jenny, who was also the cook, served the boys their lunch. Hot potato soup steaming in bowls, fresh homemade white bread cut in thick slices, was served with rich country butter.

Matthew's mouth started to water, his stomach was growling. Fresh sausages still simmered on a big meat platter. When the boys had polished off the delicious lunch, they were led back to the dormitory to settle in for the afternoon. Dinner was a repeated delight but not so heavy.

Gallio's first night at the school was plagued with trouble-some dreams of home and his mother. The next morning was dark and rainy. It seemed to foreshadow for him a dreary outlook for the rest of the summer.

As the three students got ready for the day, a buggy rolled up to the entrance of the dormitory. Voices and the banging of the front door announced the arrival of three more summer art students.

Zerby's whiny voice grouched in the hall.

"You, William Johnson, are in room four with Edward Myers. James Peabody, you share room number six with Matthew Gallio." Matthew stiffened when he heard his name mentioned.

He sat down on the edge of his bed, waiting for what came next as the door to room six creaked open slowly.

Standing in the doorway was a slight blond boy wearing gold-rimmed glasses that appeared to be magnifying-glass thick. The boy hesitated then walked toward the other empty bed in the room.

"Mmmm—Mmmm—My name is James Peabody," he stuttered.

Remembering what Father Timothy had tried to teach him about manners, Matthew extended his right hand awkwardly toward the newcomer.

"I'm Matthew Gallio from Franklinton."

"I'm James Peabody from Pittsburgh."

Matthew smiled his rare smile at James and the boy smiled shyly back. Gallio started to relax with his new roommate, feeling perhaps they could become friends.

Zerby spent the next few minutes giving his orientation speech to the new arrivals, his patience obviously wearing thin. Satisfied that he had prepared them for the day, he walked outside behind the outhouse to smoke a cigar. He'd been told not to smoke in front of the students, but he kept a good supply of cheap cigars hidden in his bureau drawer.

Classes started at 8:00 a.m. the following day.

If the orphan from Franklinton had been surprised by the grandeur of Cowan's house, he was equally surprised by the size and furnishings of the art studio in the rear of the house. It made Matthew's hands fairly itch to start working when he saw the abundance of supplies placed at each student's easel.

Cowan opened classes by explaining, "It has always been my practice to ask beginning students to use pencil on paper for their first project...to draw something from memory. Something that has impressed you. This way I can get some idea of where you are in your artistic pursuits. Are there any questions?"

James Peabody raised his hand. "Do you mm...mean we should draw something in particular that we like?"

"Anything you liked or disliked that made a strong impression on you."

Matthew fingered the fine drawing pencils in his box of supplies, then he saw the sticks of charcoal lying beside them. The paper leaned against the easel inviting him to work. Charcoal in hand, he started to draw quickly, deliberately. Bold black strokes were struck on the white and his energy was thrown at the paper. No one else was in the room for him. He stood there remembering and drawing.

A clock struck somewhere from far off in the house.

"All right, students, let's finish our pictures as soon as possible. Quickly!" Cowan clapped his hands together then walked slowly behind the first boy in the front row, Terence Bradley. "Hmmm...I see you have a flair for the dramatic." Bradley's picture of a soldier on a rearing, chestnut horse was neat and well executed.

"Good, Bradley, good!"

The teacher moved on, stopping momentarily behind two of the three other would-be artists, observing, commenting, suggesting ways to better execute their work.

When he got to James Peabody's easel, he was full of praise for the boy's drawing of a rainbow trout jumping high into the air as it was snagged by a young fisherman. James was overjoyed with the teacher's praise.

Matthew wished he could disappear. How could he compete with these people? Cowan stood behind him, silent except for one sharp intake of breath. A trio of faces stared back at him from the paper.

"Why did you use charcoal, Matthew?"

"I...I don't know. It just seemed right."

Some of the boys snickered. Gallio's face was bright red. "That's enough!" Arthur Cowan silenced the class. "You may all take a ten-minute break, except for Matthew. You come with me to my office. Bring your drawing."

"Oh Jesus!" Matthew whispered under his breath.

Once inside the office, Cowan said, "Please sit down and try to relax, son."

"I'm sorry, sir, if I did something wrong."

"WRONG! Bloody good, boy! You've done very right, as far as I can tell. Rarely do I like to evaluate a student in front of the class. This is between us."

"Yes sir." Gallio answered, not understanding.

"Those faces, son...those miners' faces....Who showed you how to draw them like that, with such fear and emotion on their faces...the stark black lines and their stricken eyes?"

"No one had to show me, Mr. Cowan. You said to draw something I remembered that was very important to me. I remember those men very well from the mine cave-in where my Pa died."

"I'm sorry to hear about your father, Matthew. It would be strange if you didn't remember. May I hold on to these drawings for a little while?"

"I guess so. I can draw more."

"Thank you, Matthew. Now let's get back to the studio."

Bradley and Plummer, expecting a chastised Gallio, were surprised when Arthur Cowan entered the classroom with his arm across Matthew's shoulder and Gallio smiling like an angel.

In the following weeks, it became increasingly obvious to Bradley and Plummer, if not the rest of the students, that Cowan held Matthew's work up as an example. James Peabody, who also shined with his beautiful depictions of birds and other wildlife, felt honored to call Gallio his friend and roommate.

Terrence Bradley's jealousy of Gallio grew each day. He openly discussed his feelings with his roommate, Plummer. "Let's get rid of the little WOP!"

Puzzled, Plummer asked, "How can we do that?"

The plan started there.

The two, Bradley and Plummer, awaited an opportunity to enter Reginald Zerby's room. They had observed Zerby's habit of smoking and guessed he hid his cigars in his room as well as other things they might steal. Their opportunity came on the fourth Sunday after their arrival.

Zerby chaperoned the boys who went to church. Matthew was unceremoniously dropped off at the Catholic Church, being the only Catholic among the students. The remainder of the students were taken by Zerby to the Methodist Church.

Bradley and Plummer begged off from church that morning, saying they were behind in their respective art projects and wished to stay working in the studio.

The students gone, they entered Zerby's room as soon as the group of churchgoers left the estate.

Opening dresser drawers, Bradley ordered, "Get the weasel's cigars."

"What'll I do with them?"

"Just hang onto them for a few seconds while I check the rest of his drawers...Well, well, well...look here! Ole Zerby's got his cash stashed under the paper liner of his shirt drawer."

"Oh Jesus! Terry, you're not going to take his money, are you?"

"You forgot, my friend, we're not taking anything, Gallio is! If he just takes the cigars he'll get off, but if he steals the money, it's all over. "Bradley stuffed the money in his pants pocket. "Let's get out of here, quick."

Plummer watched as the other boy put the cigars and money in the bottom drawer of Matthew's clothes chest, under the paper liner in the back. The two plotters then hurried to the main house and scurried into the studio as quietly as possible.

Mose pulled the rig up to the cottage after church to drop off the churchgoers, Zerby remained in the buggy, riding over to the main house. Hurriedly, the little man went to his office to catch up on some paper work. As he passed the studio door, he observed Plummer and Bradley engrossed in their work. *Good fellows,* he thought to himself as the dinner bell rang.

After dinner, Zerby headed for the cottage with plans for a smoke out back.

Opening the drawer where he kept his cigars, he knew at once that someone had been going through his belongings—and the cigars were gone.

"God dammit!" he swore to himself. Someone had stolen his smokes. His face contorted into a hateful grimace. There was nothing, immediately, that he could do about the loss without revealing to his boss that he had been smoking on the premises.

Wasting no time, he reached for the paper liner that covered his cash. The money was gone. He could do something about that.

He waited for the supper bell to ring, calling them all to eat. Hanging back, waiting for the students to file out, he then went directly to room number six. Riffling through Matthew's dresser drawers, he quickly found the money and the cigars.

"The lousy little WOP's a thief....I'll fix him."

His chest puffed out, a triumphant leer on his face, Zerby knocked on Arthur Cowan's office door.

"Come," Cowan's voice called back.

Opening the door, Zerby quickly approached his employer.

"We have a thief in our midst."

"Why, Reginald, what are you saying?"

"It's true. I have proof that Matthew Gallio is a dirty little thief. He stole from my dresser. I found the money, in the exact amount, in the bottom drawer of his dresser. It was obviously hidden in the back under his drawer liner."

"Did you, or anyone you've talked to, say that they saw Matthew steal your goods?"

"No...but it's obvious, isn't it? The little WOP had the things in his possession." Zerby's face blanched after he realized what he'd said in front of Arthur Cowan.

Cowan raised his hand for silence. "We'll have none of that kind of talk around here. You go about your business as usual; I'll handle this matter in my own way in my own time. He dismissed Zerby with a wave of his hand.

Chapter 3: Opportunists

AGATHA GLENN had watched the spring rains bring out the verdancy of the mountains, making her feel fresh and alive again as the trees whispered of summer coming. The hollyhocks, too, opened their trumpet petals, heralding the time of heat, sweat, and cool wading in the Franklinton River.

She sat in her room overlooking the town, allowing her senses to drink it all in. To renew her as it always did, away from the din of the household.

It had been two weeks since Matthew Gallio had been put on a train by Father Cassidy to attend that art school in Philadelphia. She wondered if the experience would change the boy very much. She hoped not, for she always had liked the young man and his sister.

As the mountain air wafted through her windows, she sat up straighter in her rocker, peering into the town square. *It can't be,* she thought. But sure enough, there was Teresa Gallio Bird with that young husband of hers, Jim, leading the way on a direct route to the rectory.

They approached the door and knocked on it firmly. Julia Keep's face appeared in the doorway. Jim Bird seemed to be doing all of the talking as they entered the rectory.

Agatha wrinkled her forehead in thought.

"Teresa! This is a surprise! Come in. Come in." Father Cassidy motioned them into chairs in the parlor. "And how is everything in Pittsburgh?"

Teresa looked at Jim before answering. She kept her eyes lowered and picked at her well-worn skirt. "Everything is fine, Father."

Jim Bird nudged a bony elbow into her side.

"We came to see Matthew...to take him back with us." Teresa smiled wanly.

Jim Bird nodded in agreement, his skinny cadaver-like face covered with deep acne scars.

"My, you must be doing well very fast. It's been only four months since you got married and left Franklinton. Have things picked up that much?" Father Cassidy's face was full of curiosity.

"Look, we didn't come here to chit-chat," Bird blurted.

"You shouldn't talk to the Father that way."

"Well it's true, ain't it?"

"Father, we really believe that Matthew should be with kin. So if you'll just call Matthew in here we'll be on our way back to Pittsburgh."

"Just slow down a little, Teresa, so I can get the straight of all this. You planned on coming here today and just whisking the boy, without any notice, out of here and going back to Pittsburgh?"

Teresa blushed bright red.

"And why shouldn't she. She's his only living relative and has every right to be his guardeen! You ain't got no right to stop her."

"Just a minute, son. I haven't said I'd stop her, have I? The real question in my mind is why, after such a short time, you have suddenly decided you can afford to take care of Matthew?"

"You can't fool us. We read in the Pittsburgh papers about Matthew winning that there money for his painting, and we don't intend for someone else to profit from Matthew's talent." Bird was getting mean. "You call him in here right now!"

Ignoring Bird, Father Cassidy looked into Teresa's face. "He isn't here, Teresa."

The girl was openly afraid of Jim Bird and crying. "Wh-wh-wh-where is he, Father?"

"He's away at an art school this summer."

"Oh yea? Well you just tell us where and we'll go collect the young genius."

"Jim!"

"You shut up." Bird jumped to his feet.

"Please, son, don't get excited. I'm sure we can settle this amicably. I suggest you and Teresa think this over until Matthew returns in the fall."

"We ain't waitin' til fall."

"I don't see how it can be settled before then." The priest stood up to leave the room.

Bird opened his mouth to say something more just as Julia Keep opened the parlor door.

"Father, police officer Ryan is waiting in your study to discuss the raffle for St. Joseph's new chapel glass."

Teresa was still weeping when Jim Bird shoved her through the rectory door, looking over his shoulder and vowing to return for Matthew.

Timothy Cassidy entered his study to find there was no one there. Julia stood hiding her face in her apron. "I'll see you in confession, my good woman." He patted her shoulder.

At mid-morning the next day, Teresa stood at the back door of the rectory, knocking to get Julia's attention. When the housekeeper opened the door, the girl fairly jumped into the kitchen.

"My word, child, what's happened to your eye? It's bruised."

"Nothing, nothing. I must talk to Father Cassidy quickly."

"You sit right here at the kitchen table and rest. I'll see if he's free right now."

Julia found the priest in the sanctuary. "Father, Teresa Bird is in the kitchen waiting to talk to you. It seems to be very important."

The old priest kneeled before the altar, genuflected, crossed himself, and hurried out of the church. Julia followed.

"She looks hurt to me, Father. Her left eye is badly swollen."

"You bring her into my study."

When Teresa saw Father Cassidy, she threw herself to her knees in front of him, sobbing and moaning. It reminded him of the last time she'd gone to her knees in the same room, when the two had planned for Matthew's future.

"Please, Teresa, don't cry like that. It can't be that bad."

"But it is, Father. I've come to warn you about Jim Bird. He ain't rested a minute ever since he found out about my brother making that money and getting all that notice from the high muckity-mucks in Philadelphia. He has plans to make Matthew do drawings for him to sell. I sneaked away this morning by telling him I would visit a few minutes with Mrs. Glenn."

"Surely you must understand that your brother is just a student of the art of painting. He's in no position to make money for anyone yet."

"Jim don't understand none of that. He's just seein' dollar signs where Matthew is concerned. Please, Father, no matter what I'm forced to say, you must not give Matthew over to us. It would be a terrible existence for him. If you care for my brother, you'll fix it so he'll never leave your control 'til he's on his own."

I understand, Teresa, but what about you? Things look pretty bad for you. Does he beat you?"

"That ain't important now. I can take care of myself. Just promise me you'll keep Matthew."

"I'll do my best, child."

"If Jim Bird finds out I've been here, he'll probably try to kill me."

"I promise never to let him know about our meeting."

The girl left by the back door of the rectory, the same way she came.

The priest sat at his desk for a long time after she left. He thought about the bargain he'd made with her, and about the last few months of joy the boy had given to him. All in all, he decided he'd had the best of the deal. He loved Matthew as the son he'd never had. How could he ever put the boy into the environment that Jim Bird had in mind? Bird was obviously heaping abuse on Teresa and would, no doubt, do the same with Matthew.

Legally, he feared he had no right to keep Matthew from his sister, but he knew it would hurt the boy if he turned him over. There had to be a way he could ensure the child's security, at least until he was of age. In this case, he could be no Solomon.

Fred Slager sat in his office in the First Union Bank, looking out the window. His slate grey eyes followed the progress of Timothy Cassidy as he hurried along the street toward the bank. Slager wore two hats in town. He was the attorney for Glenn Enterprises and the president of the bank. As he observed the priest, huffing and puffing his way into the bank entrance, he knew there must be trouble afoot for his old friend.

The little wooden gate that separated the main lobby of the small bank from Slager's office flew inward as Father Cassidy pushed his way into the banker's office.

"Timothy! What brings you out among the heathen on a beautiful day like this?" He extended his big hand across his desk to the priest. His habit of not rising had nothing to do with a lack of manners but more to do with his girth, which encircled his three hundred pounds.

"Fred, it's a blessing to have a good friend like you to come to in time of need."

"You know I'm here if I can be of service to you. What's up? Does the sanctuary roof leak?"

"It might be better if it was that simple. No, this is a problem about my ward, Matthew Gallio. It's crucial that I get legal custody of the boy, and quickly."

"I thought that was a temporary arrangement with the boy's sister. Am I wrong?"

Slowly and carefully, Father Cassidy explained the happenings of the day to Slager. When he had repeated all of the conversations with the Birds, he ended, saying, "You can see why I can't walk away from this."

The banker moved his pudgy hands slowly over the papers on his desk, adjusting them here and there in silence. After a minute or two he said, "Can you give me until day after tomorrow? Judge Tinsdale is over in the valley at Fiddler's Creek this week for a trial. I can send my assistant over there in the morning with the necessary papers for him to sign."

Julia Keep couldn't ignore the sound of pacing back and forth that came from the rectory study the next morning. Neither could she ignore the fact that the Birds had sent a note to the priest saying that they would be at the rectory at 4:00 p.m. that day. Again they requested the address of the school where Matthew was enrolled. The look on the Father's face when he read the note spoke volumes about his misery.

The good Father finally slammed out of his study, heading for the front door. He called back to Julia that he would be out of town until the next morning. The last she saw of him he was driving his horse and buggy out of the livery stable, headed north toward Bear Mountain.

The weather held sunny as the buggy rattled off twelve miles over the mountain to Coalport. He would stay overnight at the small rectory for traveling priests that was in the coal town.

When Jim Bird and Teresa arrived at St. Joseph's promptly at four o'clock, Julia could do nothing more than tell them that Father Cassidy would be gone until the next day.

Bird reacted with a curse, while shaking his fist in Julia's face. He told her they'd be back the next day fully expecting the priest to comply with their demands.

During the last mile of Timothy Cassidy's journey back to Franklinton, it was pouring rain. A gloomy day, he thought, for a gloomy deed. When he arrived back home, the housekeeper handed him a fat brown envelope with a wax seal on the flap. It was a statement from the circuit judge saying that permanent custody of one Matthew Gallio, born August 10, 1840, was awarded to the Right Reverend Timothy Q. Cassidy on this day, July 11, 1853.

How Fred Slager managed the whole thing so swiftly was a mystery to the priest, but he wouldn't question it.

The Birds arrived on the doorstep of the rectory that afternoon, wet from pouring rain and in a hurry. Julia ushered them into the study where they stood looking at Father Cassidy, who wore an angelic smile.

"Ah, children, your arrival has been anticipated. Will you sit down?"

"Naw, we ain't sittin'. Just give us the kid's address."

"I deeply regret that I must inform you that I have taken steps that make Matthew Gallio my ward, legally and permanently, until he is of age. I must also inform you that any steps taken by either of you, at this time, to interfere with the boy's life will be illegal and apt to land you in a court of law. I further suggest that the two of you go back to Pittsburgh and resume your pursuit of a decent life for yourselves. In the meantime, if you wish to *see* your brother, Teresa, at a later date, I will entertain a request for a meeting between the two of you whenever it is best for Matthew. Now I think you had better hurry for the five o'clock train to Pittsburgh."

Jim Bird and Teresa stood with their mouths pinched shut as Julia gently nudged them toward the door.

When they were gone, Timothy Cassidy pulled out the lower drawer of his desk, reached in and retrieved a bottle of well-aged whiskey. He poured three fingers of the whiskey into a glass, telling himself that he must remember to offer Fred Slager the other bottle, secreted under a pile of papers in the same drawer. What better gift could he offer his friend?

He'd have to write Matthew and tell him that his home was now secure for him for a long time. He hoped.

Chapter 4: Treachery

MONDAY MORNING, as the art class began its work, Matthew was summoned to Arthur Cowan's office. He walked into the office and was asked by Cowan to close the door.

Zerby was in Cowan's office, sitting in a straight-backed chair facing the teacher's desk.

Arthur Cowan beckoned Matthew to enter and be seated. The teacher's face was stern and pale, with a worried line between his eyes.

Zerby, his full lips moist, had a self-satisfied look on his face.

Looking from one man to the other, Matthew felt as if he were being offered up as a sacrifice to some vengeful god.

Arthur Cowan faced Matthew with troubled eyes. "I have heard some very serious allegations against you, but before I act on the accusations, I want to hear your explanation of things."

"I don't understand, sir."

"I think you do," Zerby interjected.

"I'll handle this, Mr. Zerby." The teacher scowled. "Yesterday, Mr. Zerby discovered some of his money missing from the shirt drawer of his dresser. Following his own instincts, he proceeded to search the cottage for likely clues as to whoever could have stolen it.

Sadly, I must say, he found the missing money in the drawer of your dresser under the paper liner!"

Matthew looked stricken. "Sir, I didn't take any money or anything else from Mr. Zerby's room."

"That's what we must be sure of, Matthew. Unfortunately, we have only your word against Mr. Zerby's. Is there any way you see that you can prove you are not the guilty party?"

"I don't know. I'd have to think about it. When did the money disappear, sir?"

Zerby jumped in again. "I discovered it gone after I returned to the cottage just at dinner time. You were there the whole time that I was working after church."

"So were a lot of other students," Matthew answered. "Yes, but I didn't find the money in 'other students' dresser drawers, I found it in yours."

"James was with me the whole time after church. You can ask him." Matthew's face was ashen.

"Very well, Matthew, we will ask him," Cowan agreed. "But surely you must see that alone won't be enough to exonerate you. After all, James is a good friend of yours and just might lie to aid his friend."

"I don't believe James would lie for anyone, sir."

"Nevertheless, we will have to do some further investigating on the matter and if it turns out that we cannot prove you innocent, I will be forced to send you home with the bad news that you've been expelled from the school. I'm seriously hoping that will not happen." Cowan motioned for the boy to leave the room while turning his attention to Zerby.

"You, Mr. Zerby, are to leave any further pursuit of this matter to me and me alone. Do you understand?"

Under his breath he said, "Coddling the little WOP."

"What did you say, Zerby?"

"Nothing, sir."

Matthew, too upset to work and feeling ill, went back to his room at the cottage.

James came to the room at lunch break to see what had happened to his friend. The whole story was retold by Matthew. "It looks like someone's doing this to me on purpose."

"Well, I was with you the whole t-t-t-time after church. In fact, I don't thu-thu-think we left the room until we went up to the house for dinner. I'll tell them the truth and they'll f-f-forget this f-f-foolishness."

"I'm afraid it's much more serious than that. Zerby seems to be bent on getting me ousted."

"How can Mr. Cowan do that? He knows you're a gifted artist already."

"Now, James, I thank you for your loyalty but I'm afraid that even if what you say is true, I'm going to need more than your say-so to clear myself." He threw himself onto his bed with a moan.

"We'll do our b-b-best and I know it'll t-t-turn out to be all right in the end. It has to!" James Peabody offered Matthew his hand once again.

Arthur had each and every one of the students into his office on Tuesday...one at a time. None of them seemed to have anything to add to help Gallio's story except James. Cowan felt that Plummer was overly nervous about the interview but put it down to anxiety over the incident.

By Wednesday, Arthur Cowan had to make the painful decision to expel Matthew from the school forever. He called Gallio in.

While Matthew made his way to the house from the cottage, James Peabody was announcing to all of the students in the studio that, perhaps, the most gifted of all of them was going to be banished for something he could not have done and if he ever found out who did this thing, he would set matters straight with dire consequences. He hardly stuttered at all.

Cowan had just delivered his private edict to Gallio. "You have no idea the pain this causes me, but I have no alternate path to take. You must know that I consider you one of the most gifted students I have ever had here at Cowan House. I also want you to know that I personally believe you but have no proof to allow for clemency to you."

Matthew rose with tears streaming down his face and an ache in his chest. "When will I be sent home?"

"We'll send you to the station with Mose tomorrow afternoon."

"If you'll excuse me, sir, I'll go and begin to pack my things. Before I go I want you to know that I didn't want to come here this summer, but now it has become very important to me. I've already learned so much. Thank you."

He turned to leave. There was a light tap at the door. Cowan went to the door himself and opened it. Standing there in the hallway were James Peabody and Jonathan Plummer.

"Yes boys, what is it?"

"I think that Jonathan has something to say to you and M-M-Matthew." He gave Plummer a gentle shove.

"Come in, Jonathan. Sit down." Cowan indicated the chair across from Matthew's.

James stayed back in the hall, waiting by the closed door. There was confusion in the small office as the three moved around the desk to be seated. Plummer was red in the face and seemed to be very agitated.

"You have interrupted a highly important meeting here, Mr. Plummer. I hope that what you have come to say is illuminating."

"Yes sir! I believe it's important, or I wouldn't have interfered in this meeting."

"Come come, Plummer, let's get on with it."

"I have come to tell you that Matthew had nothing to do with the disappearance of Mr. Zerby's goods and money."

"How, may I ask, do you happen to know this?"

"Because I was there and was part of the joke."

"JOKE! Did you say JOKE?" I assure you, Plummer, this is no JOKE. Just tell me what this is all about."

"Well, Terrence Bradley and I thought it might be fun to get Matthew in trouble with Mr. Zerby, seeing as how he didn't like Matthew much anyway. So Terrence figured out a way to get Matthew in trouble with Zerby. I didn't know in the beginning that it would get so serious.

"Please...just tell me what happened."

Plummer, holding his head down, looked at Matthew from under lowered eyelids. "I told Terence not to touch the money!" His fists hit his knees in a self-inflicted tattoo. "He said we'd just take Zerby's cigars and then he got the idea to steal the money, too, when he saw it in the same drawer."

"When did all of this occur?" Cowan leaned forward.

"We stayed home from church by saying we were behind in our projects in the studio. Then we sneaked down to the cottage. That was after everyone left in the buggy with Mose."

"The cigars were Mr. Zerby's?"

"Yes sir. He smokes them behind the outhouse."

"Matthew, please go back to the cottage and prepare yourself for your classes tomorrow." Arthur Cowan patted the boy's shoulder when he stood.

Alone with Plummer, he told him to sit there while he sent for Terrence Bradley. He did not call for Zerby.

When Bradley entered the teacher's office, he knew the truth was out but continued to smirk in a supercilious manner.

"Are you finding something amusing, Mr. Bradley?"

Terrence Bradley gave no answer; he just shrugged.

"Jonathan tells me that the two of you are responsible for the theft of Mr. Zerby's money. Is that true?"

"I guess you could say that, but we didn't really steal it, we just *moved* it." He grinned.

"The very act of removing it from Mr. Zerby's drawer to someone else's property is, in fact, a theft. I'm truly sorry such a mean-spirited thing has occurred in my school. We have never had such a thing happen here before. Have you got anything further to add to this mess?"

Again, Bradley just shrugged and grinned.

Plummer had broken down completely and was crying.

"You, Terrence Bradley, are despicable. Even more so by your actions in this office. At least Jonathan has the decency to know how wrong he was and have some remorse, something that seems to elude you.

"The two of you will pack your belongings this evening and you will be sent home on tomorrow's afternoon train. A full explanation of this matter will be sent to your parents. You will not be welcome in this school again. You're dismissed."

Back at the cottage the students were quietly waiting for the arrival of the two thieves to find out their punishment.

Plummer quietly entered the room he shared with Bradley, while the troublemaker, Bradley, stood in the hallway loudly declaring that the only thing he was sorry about was that he hadn't gotten rid of the "dirty little WOP."

James Peabody ran out of his room with his fists held up. "You take that back, you thief!"

Bradley turned around just in time to hit James with all his might, right between the eyes, knocking James's glasses to the floor where they shattered.

It happened so fast that Matthew hardly got out of his room in time to see the melee. He hurried to help James up as Bradley tried pummeling him over the head. Once James was out of the fray, Matthew turned on Bradley, striking him first in the nose, which bled profusely, then socking him in the eye.

Bradley backed up toward his room as Matthew allowed his fury to be unleashed on his enemy at last. A bloodied Terrence Bradley ran into his room and locked the door as the rest of the boys cheered.

The only mark on Gallio was a slight cut above his left eyebrow, which Mose tended to that night. It seemed that Mose had been put in charge of the cottage until a new assistant could be hired at Cowan House. Reginald Zerby was asked to take his cigars and leave the next day with Plummer and a very quiet Bradley. Mose drove the three travelers to the railroad station. He sat, unmoving, as the three departed carrying their own bags.

Chapter 5: Illumination

SUMMER SIZZLED its way through August in Philadelphia. Young Matthew Gallio settled into a routine of work and even some pleasure. He found the schedule at Cowan's motivating and enjoyed the new friendships he had formed with James Peabody and the other students. Even his relationship with Arthur Cowan was rewarded not only by the teacher's respect for his work but with Cowan's friendship.

Matthew liked the picnics on the terrace each Sunday evening, weather permitting, and the sounds of music from the piano in the parlor, when Arthur Cowan sometimes played. He was growing accustomed to the different lifestyle that prevailed at Cowan House.

After the incident involving the theft and the ultimate dismissal of the two boys, along with Reginald Zerby's dismissal, Matthew's days were filled with a kaleidoscope of learning. How to handle colors, the hue, intensity, shading, and style as related to form, content, and values were taught. Many other aspects of the fine art of painting were to be touched upon in depth at later sessions.

It was during just such a lesson period on the effects of distance in a painting, as related to the use of paler, less intense color for far away objects, that the class was interrupted by the arrival of an important guest. Mose quietly informed Cowan that Mrs. Clarinda Bartholomew was awaiting his presence in the front parlor.

Arthur quickly gave the students instructions on their assignment and left the classroom.

Entering the parlor, he brushed a hand over his hair and touched his blond-gray mustache.

Rising slightly from the tapestry settee, then reseating herself, Clarinda Bartholomew opened her arms wide to accept Arthur's kiss on her pink cheek. Seated beside her, observing all of this, was a young girl with golden hair. She looked squarely at Arthur with eyes the color of summer skies. The girl smiled up at him impishly, showing her perfect white teeth.

"My dear, how lovely you look." Arthur caught Clarinda's small hands in his and kissed them tenderly. The diamonds of her several rings glittered in the afternoon sunlight. At sixty, she was still a beautiful woman, neatly packaged, if slightly plump. Her angelic white hair, belying her auburn-haired temperament, suited her lovely face. She was wearing a deep purple cambric summer suit. Its basque waist was corseted to a lovely curve, matching the slightly bustled and draped skirt that reached to her ankles, revealing small black ankle-high shoes. On her head she'd pinned a small straw bonnet with matching purple ribbons and a few dried flowers.

Arthur stared at Clarinda as if she were a prized Rembrandt. His face was red, a curse he suffered every time he was in Clarinda's presence. He pulled a white silk handkerchief from his breast pocket and pressed it to his forehead before replacing it.

"This must be your granddaughter I've heard so much about. Dear child, you are as lovely as your grandmother." The girl giggled.

"Arienne, this is the famous artist-teacher Arthur Cowan." The child, who looked to be about twelve years old, stood up and straightened her full white skirts, then daintily curtsied to Cowan.

Clarinda's dark eyes wandered up to the painting over the mantel. The young girl in the painting, wearing the blue dress, seemed to look down lovingly on all.

"Arthur, must you keep that painting forever on public view? It only serves to remind me how old I am."

"You will never be old, my dear."

"Nonsense! Of course I'm getting old."

"How is your son Gerald these days? I see his name often in the paper."

"He's running around making deals everywhere, as always. He never stops. Sometimes I think he's driven by a devil."

Mose entered the room with tea on a silver tray. Setting it on a low table near Clarinda, he prepared to serve.

"Never mind, Moses. I know you have much to do...I'll pour." Clarinda dismissed him with a sweet smile.

"That will be all, Mose." Arthur gave the server a wink.

The teacher seated himself by the other side of Clarinda on the settee.

"Take some cookies, Arienne, and go out and look at the garden for a few minutes. Arthur and I want to talk."

The girl picked up some cookies and walked through the French doors toward the terrace. She was glad to be excused from the adult conversation.

Clarinda poured two cups of tea. The two sipped in silence for a minute.

"Do you know that I still feel the same way about you, as I did when I painted that portrait of you?"

"Now Arthur, you certainly didn't beckon me to your side today to wax romantic after all these years." Her eyes sparkled.

"How many times have I asked you to marry me since Chester Bartholomew passed on...ten, twelve times?"

"And how many times in the last ten years have I told you, old friend, that I will never marry again?"

"It seems your father was right, long ago, when he told you that it wasn't possible for you to be in love with a poor artist like I was. If you'd have really cared for me, nothing would have kept us apart...not even your rich father!"

"Enough of this kind of talk, Arthur. It serves no purpose. Anyway, it all happened for the best. Look what you've accomplished in your career."

Arthur chuckled a little and got to his feet. "Still the evasive one, my dear!" He paced a bit.

"Let's get back to why you sent for me."

"You remember the small painting you bought from the winner of the French Award? The young artist that lives in Franklinton—his name is Gallio."

"Yes, of course I remember. I've hung that painting in my bedroom. If his parents or someone wants to buy it back, tell them it's not for sale!"

"No, nothing like that, Clarinda, the boy is here for my summer session for juniors. I thought you might like to see some of his work, since you liked his entry so much."

"Ah, **I** feel a patron-of-the-arts plea coming on!"

"Not necessarily. I just want you to look."

"Well, let's get on with it." She stood and brushed imaginary wrinkles from her skirt.

Arthur led the way to his private study. He seated Clarinda as far back from his desk as possible. Holding Matthew's charcoal drawings up one at a time, he held them over his desk for her to see.

As Clarinda sat there, she leaned closer to the drawings, as if memorizing them. "How old is this young man?"

"He's thirteen years old."

"I hardly know what to say, Arthur. These do not look like the work of a child. Are you sure they're his?"

"I promise you they are. I was in the studio as he worked on them."

"This talent can't be wasted." She spoke with authority.

"Exactly my thoughts. The problem is the boy's practically an orphan. He's being given a home by the local Catholic priest in Franklinton. There is little or no money to pay for him to study. Your purchase of his painting made it possible for him to be here this summer."

"Can't you give him a scholarship, Arthur? It seems to me you could do that."

"I intend to do that very thing, but the boy needs further financial aid for proper clothes, more education, and a stipend for after he graduates from secondary school. I hope to keep him out of the mines. If he goes to work in the mines, he'll never reach his potential."

"Who looks after his needs now?"

"The old priest he lives with is his legal guardian. He's done well by the boy, but he's not able to give him much more than room and board."

Arienne strolled into the study, the front of her dress muddy, her face bright. She carried a handful of marigolds in one hand and a batch of petunias in the other. "See what I picked for you, Grandmother. Aren't they just beautiful?"

"Honestly, Arienne, I don't know what to do with you. Imagine you picking Arthur's flowers right out of his garden... and your dress is ruined!"

"Oh, poo! This old dress is too hot anyway." She went to Clarinda and laid the flowers in her grandmother's lap, kissing the old lady's cheek.

"See, Arthur, I have no control at all." Her black eyes danced. Her love for the motherless child of her only son shown from her eyes.

The girl left them alone again as she wandered back outside.

"Gerald adores the child but spends little time with her. He likes to see her dressed to the nines, especially for church. When she sits beside him in the pew, he seems to almost burst with pride. She depends on me for her companionship, though. Sometimes it's a bit much for me, chasing after a twelve-year-old."

"Why doesn't Gerald hire a governess?"

"He'd never allow an outsider to raise her. He's a very possessive man. But then he always was. When I think about the way he used to shadow her mother before the child was born, I shudder. When Ariene's mother died in childbirth, he was inconsolable for months. Ah well, let's not fret about the past. What do you want me to do about the Gallio boy?"

"I was thinking, perhaps, a modest monthly stipend until he's eighteen and producing enough to keep himself. I believe he will be very successful."

"It's a slight gamble, but I like to gamble once in a while. I'd like to meet the young man before I decide."

Lunch over, Arthur led Clarinda and Arienne out on the terrace to a shady table and chairs. He excused himself and went to get Matthew. Arthur and Matthew walked out onto the terrace talking.

Clarinda watched the two approach. The young man was tall for his age, and still slightly built. His beautiful black hair curled tightly in the summer humidity. He was a handsome boy, she thought. His dark good looks were to her liking, and his steel blue eyes looked into hers levelly.

Arienne was watching Arthur and Matthew approach. She suddenly became very shy.

The meeting was a special one for all that day.

Matthew found Clarinda to be a charming, warm, and interesting lady. His opinion of the girl who stared at him almost constantly was one of amusement and appreciation for the small girl's beauty, even if she was slightly muddy here and there.

As for Clarinda Bartholomew, she lost her heart to the young artist.

Chapter 6: Obsessions

AGATHA GLENN'S two children were very different. The oldest, Jordan, was by far the handsomest child in his class at school. His pale blond beauty was noticed by all from the day he was born. People stopped Agatha on the narrow sidewalks when she pushed the big wicker baby buggy to tell her what a beautiful child he was. They meant it.

Some in town wondered out loud where the boy got his good looks. Certainly not from Conrad, the father, whose round ruddy features were anything but handsome, and Agatha was really rather plain in her beige-brown way. Brown hair, brown eyes, and even her skin was a beigey tone. Women artists would probably see her in sepia, if they saw her at all. Her main attribute, which she passed on to Jordan, was her height. She was nearly six feet tall, overshadowing her husband by two inches.

Jordan Glenn was Agatha's favorite. She spoiled him badly. Her failure to discipline the boy was obvious to all except Agatha. She consoled herself with the lie that the mischief Jordan caused was just him "being a boy."

At eight, he set the utility shed on fire playing with matches. Agatha excused that by saying it was the cook's fault for having matches within the children's reach. She fired the cook with Jordan looking on from behind her skirts.

"I'm so sorry, Mama," he whimpered as she stooped to embrace his small, perfect little body. He hugged her long neck smiling at the cook over his mother's shoulder. The cook stood mute, utterly dismayed at the child's lack of conscience.

Agatha was just relieved that the child was not injured. Nothing else mattered. All of the troubles Jordan caused were just "natural" boy things, after all.

One of the things not quite "natural" was his very early attraction to the opposite sex.

Dolly Glenn, eighteen months younger than her twelve-year-old brother, raced up the steps to the tower room screaming, crying for her mother. The child was disheveled and her face was scratched. She flung herself into Agatha's arms.

"Ma, Ma! Jordan hurt me. He got me down and beat on me..."

"Whoa! Now, darling, take a deep breath and tell me what you mean. I'm sure Jordan didn't mean to hurt you."

"Yes he did. He did! He's tried to hurt me before."

"Surely it's not that bad." Agatha's face was indulgent, showing little concern.

"He knocked me down and tried to take my underpants off. I told you before how he tried to do that."

Agatha patted Dolly's shoulder and hugged the girl to her.

"Jordan is just a little rough, I know. I don't think he *really* wanted to hurt you, dear. He just has a lot of energy to burn."

"But he's always trying to get me alone to show me his...his..."

"Never mind, darling. I'll speak to him again. He's just a natural boy."

With that Dolly started to wail in frustration. "You always say that! You never punish Jordan for anything." She stomped one small, foot.

"Of course I do. I'll make him stay in his room tomorrow, after school."

"I'm gonna tell Daddy what Jordan does to me." It was a threat Dolly had used before but never followed through on.

"No! Daddy's too busy for such small problems."

"Someday I'm gonna get even with Jordan. Someday I'll make him stop hurting me, you'll see." She stomped away, her dark, auburn curls bobbing up and down fiercely as she kicked the back of each step on the way downstairs from Agatha's room.

****

The tower room was warm with sunshine. The curtains danced softly at the open windows, making soft whispering sounds as the breeze snapped them to and fro.

Agatha loved this time of the year almost as much as spring. It was late summer, and the cold nip of fall was on the breeze. The hills were just beginning to take on their autumnal hues. Some golds and reds peeked through the green here and there. There would be a riotous scramble of colors in just a couple of weeks.

Leaning forward in her favorite rocker, she looked down on the town square. Jordan rode out of the livery stable on Saber, his beautiful chestnut stallion. He trotted the horse up the street toward shantytown. Cutting a fine figure on a horse, at fifteen he was an expert horseman. Agatha watched her son traveling up the road, raising a dust cloud. But why was he going to the miner's part of town?

When he reached shantytown, Jordan slowed. The low tarpaper shacks hugged the dirt with a look of hopelessness. Still in sight, Jordan stopped in front of one of the hovels. A young girl with brilliant, red hair came out. She stood looking up into Jordan's face. Agatha couldn't see very clearly, but she knew that red hair. It was fifteen-year-old Goldy Wojna, daughter of one of the Glenn miners.

Anger spread over Agatha's face. Jordan had been forbidden to mix with the miner's families. How could he dare go against his father's and her wishes. Her thin face paled. She couldn't tolerate that. Conrad would have to be brought into this. Making that decision, she was to quickly change her mind when she saw Jordan gallop away from the brief encounter with Goldy. Perhaps she had taken the meeting too seriously.

****

Goldy, a ragged shawl hugged around her small body, stood stiff and frightened in the dark doorway behind the livery stable. The mountains looked black and forbidding under a clouded moon.

A whisper, "Are you there Goldy?"

"Yes."

"I see you decided to come after all."

The girl shivered. "I never stand you up, Jordan, but Pa's gonna skin me if I don't get back soon. I think he's getting suspicious of my evening walks. Maybe I won't be able to meet you anymore."

The boy laughed at her, mimicked her in a falsetto voice. *Maybe I won't come anymore!* Sez who? One word from me to my father about the way you seduced me and your old man will be out of work!"

"I never seduced nobody. Please Jordan...I didn't mean I won't come. Honest, Jordan. Please don't get Pa fired!"

"Oh puhleeze, Jordan," he repeated as he struck Goldy across the face. Her nose started to bleed as he threw her onto the ground. He was strong, brutal as he forced himself on her. Goldy wept in silence, biting her lower lip until it, too, bled.

When Agatha's pride and joy walked through the back door that night, his mother was having a cup of tea at the kitchen table. She saw the blood all over the front of his shirt.

"My, word! Whatever did you do to yourself?"

"Nothing Ma. I just had a little nose bleed and it got all over me before I realized it. You remember how I used to get those when I was little. Well, I had another one. It isn't anything...it's stopped."

Agatha sat quiet as Jordan made his way up the back stairs to his room. She felt a curious uneasiness.

****

Matthew returned from Philadelphia after spending his third summer studying with Arthur Cowan. Each time he returned, Father Cassidy could see changes in him. Not just the obvious growing up, but a difference in Matthew himself. A steadiness, more focused on his painting, and a *nice* gentle maturity that only the old priest noticed. There was a purposeful step to Matthew's walk, a self-esteem not there before, and he had grown tall...six feet, at least. He was slim like his mother.

This third fall, Matthew came back to Franklinton to enter his senior year in school. He continued to work for Bean's Grocery Store, no longer delivering but helping to run the store. The stipend that arrived each month from his secret benefactor helped him to pay his bills and put a little away.

School came easy for Matthew. Not so for Jordan Glenn, who had little interest in school.

Goldy Wojna was a very good student. She felt compelled to keep her ugly, shameful secret about her relationship with Jordan Glenn. She hated him and the things he did to her, but her fear for her family far outweighed her desire to get revenge on her abuser. Only Father Timothy seemed to notice that she was in turmoil.

"Tell me if you're in some kind of trouble, Goldy."

"I ain't in any trouble, Father. Really, I'm all right." She hated lying to Father Cassidy.

Her adoration for Matthew Gallio was another secret she dared not allow anyone to know. What good did it do for her to love Gallio? He'd never want a girl like her...used merchandise. Matthew had asked her to pose for him on two separate occasions.

"I can't pay you much for your time, but I'd like to paint you and that glorious hair."

"I can't, Pa wouldn't like it," was her excuse both times. She held his compliment about her hair close to her heart. *If he only knew how much I'd give to spend that time with him,* she thought, but Jordan might punish her for it.

Chapter 7: Changes

HALLOWEEN was approaching. The weather, usually cold enough for a coat, was unseasonably warm. Goldy was again ordered by Jordan Glenn to meet him in the dark livery stable.

"Goldy are you here?" Jordan lit a match and held it high.

Goldy cowered in a far corner, away from the horses. She was afraid of horses.

Jordan lingered in the front of Saber's stall. The spirited stallion fussed nervously. "Come here, Goldy," Jordan ordered.

"Please, Jordan, you know I'm scared of horses."

"I said come here!" He thumped the wall beside the horse with his fist. The horse reared up hitting the sides of his stall.

Goldy, her shawl wrapped closely around her shoulders, moved slowly toward Jordan. "I told you, I'm scared of horses." Her green eyes glistened with unshed tears.

"Oh dear, is the little tramp going to cry?" He mocked her.

Pulling her small shoulders back, she stood as tall as possible. "I warn't a tramp 'til you made me one. If I'm a tramp, then I guess I'm your tramp." She spit in his face.

Rage turned his eyes wild as he slapped her full-handed across the face then jerked her, mouth bleeding, into Saber's area. Saber reared again, striking the girl's left shoulder with one hoof, knocking her to the ground. Pain ran through her arm and back. She cried out. Jordan held his hand over her mouth, pulling her toward a corner of the stable. He took her there on the mud floor as she fainted. When she came around, he was gone. She lay on the stable floor half conscious.

Matthew strolled along the main street enjoying an evening walk in the moonlight. As he passed the livery stable, he heard a low moan. Entering the dark building he couldn't see anyone. Then the sound came again. "Help me, please help me."

He made out a form on the ground. Rushing over, he knelt over Goldy, her face covered with blood. "My God, Goldy, what's happened to you? Here let me help you. Can you sit up? Lean on me. I'll get you home. Who could do this?" All Goldy would answer to his questions was, "I don't know."

When Ed Wojna saw his daughter, he flew into a rage. "Who did this to you, girl?"

"I don't know...it was too dark to *see*."

Matthew thought about how bright the moon had lit up the night and knew she was lying.

She kept to her story. Although her injuries were serious, they were not life threatening. The mark that the horse left crushed into her shoulder she would carry to her grave.

****

Snow arrived in the mountains early that year, the first of November. The town was bustling. The coming of the holidays always seemed to breathe new life into the community.

Matthew kept busy at the grocery store and painting. He was asked by Agatha Glenn if he thought he could paint a portrait of herself in time for Christmas. She wanted it as a present for Conrad. A surprise!

"Something not too formal, Matthew, just a nice picture of me the way I look when I'm at my best."

"That won't be hard, Miz Glenn, and if you don't like it, you don't have to pay me for it."

"Fair enough!" she agreed.

Because the painting was a secret kept from the whole Glenn family, the sittings took place at the end of the big kitchen in the rectory. Large windows at either side supplied good light.

Agatha arrived dressed in her best silk dress. Tiny rosebuds were embroidered down the front placket. The full skirt flowed softly in waves of royal blue draped over a slight hoop. The top of the gown was pale beige and reflected no color onto her face.

"Uh, Mrs. Glenn, I really feel the color of your bodice will make your lovely portrait too drab. Some color next to your face would be nice. Something a little rosy?"

"I have never thought I could wear bright colors well with my complexion. This is my favorite dress. Certainly it will do. Don't you think?"

That settled it. Matthew struggled to make the portrait as interesting and as colorful as possible. He worked on it several weeks. When it was finished, Matthew first showed it to Agatha. He felt unsure of himself and his ability. He was always his own worst critic.

Agatha stood in the rectory kitchen staring at the large canvas on the artist's easel. Julia Keep looked on, a wide smile of pride on her face. "Oh! My, my!" Julia murmured, then checked herself.

A slight blush of color flashed across Agatha's face.

The woman staring back at her from the canvas was not beautiful; her features were sharp and thin, but somewhere in the depth of the rich brown eyes there was a loveliness of expression. The normally drab brown hair had just a hint of light auburn shining in it here and there that seemed to compliment the colors in the dress somehow.

"It will do, Matthew." She handed him seventy-five dollars. After making arrangements for framing and delivery, she quietly left, her brown eyes shining.

Matthew never mentioned the addition of the titian coloring to her hair, and neither did she.

After Christmas, the Glenn portrait became the talk of the small town. All of the ladies vied for invitations to visit Agatha for tea so that they could view the Gallio picture of her that hung over the mantel in the parlor. The general opinion was that it looked just like her, but they were piqued to find out what he had done to bring out the spiritual light that showed in her face.

Gallio would paint most of the Glenn family in his lifetime. All except Jordan.

****

Sometime after the first of the new year, 1858, a heavy blizzard hit Franklinton, bringing the town to a standstill.

Father Cassidy was in the kitchen having a cup of tea with Julia presiding. Matthew was in his room working. A light knock sounded at the back door. Hurriedly Julia opened the door to admit Goldy Wojna. The girl was standing there looking nearly frozen in a sweater and shawl, her only outer garments, neither of which was warm enough for the weather.

"Come in, come in, dear child! What are you doing in this weather?"

Father Timothy bustled around her, taking her shawl and hanging it over an old wooden kitchen chair.

Goldy's face looked pinched and pale. Even her lustrous red hair seemed to have lost its lights. She stumbled toward the table. Julia helped her into a chair. Quickly the housekeeper placed a hot cup of tea in front of the girl.

"I must talk to you, Father."

"Of course...of course we'll talk, but first get yourself warmed up a bit before you get pneumonia."

After they had settled her down a bit, she drank a portion of the hot tea.

"Come on into my office, Goldy, we can talk there." He led the girl into the study. "Now what could be so important that would bring you out on a day like this?"

"I am fearsome afraid, Father..." She started to cry. "What could possibly make such a lovely girl like you so afraid?"

"I have sinned, and now I will pay for that sin!"

"Now, now, Goldy, tell me what's wrong."

"I'm going to have a baby, Father, and if my Pa finds out, he'll kill me for sure."

"Whose child is it?

"I can't tell that. If I tell, it will make matters even worse for me."

"You can trust me, child. I have taken a sacred vow. I cannot tell."

With that, the girl seemed to crumble before his eyes and all her defenses fell away as she told the good priest of the torment she had been enduring for so long from Jordan Glenn.

Father Timothy's face went scarlet. "This is Jordan Glenn's doing?"

"Yes, Father, but no one must ever know he is the father. He has threatened me by telling me he would have Pa fired. He will deny he had anything to do with it."

The old man sat for a long time in silence as the girl wept quietly in the chair opposite him. "You must do as I tell you, child. Go home and do not tell anyone what you have told me today. As soon as I can, I'll send for you and we will settle this...somehow."

****

The huge grandfather clock in the hall at the Glenn's ticked off the time in the big house. The silence seemed heavy to Timothy Cassidy as he sat waiting for Agatha to make her appearance for their appointment. The clock struck two, breaking the stillness. Father Cassidy fidgeted in the leather easy chair.

Agatha came into the room in a flurry, her petticoats rustling, as she reached for the priest's chubby hand. "How nice, if unexpected, to see you, Father.

"Always nice seeing you, Agatha."

"What can I do for you?"

"I wish there was some easy way for me to tell you what I've come about, but there isn't."

"My! It must be serious."

"It is serious."

After standing through the greetings, Agatha sat down abruptly across from him in a matching chair.

"I have come to tell you that your son, Jordan, has gotten one of the girls in trouble."

"Oh come now, Father Timothy...that's hard for me to believe."

"You can believe it, Agatha."

"And just who is making these accusations?"

"Before I tell you who, I am going to tell you what your son has been up to for the past year and a half." The priest sat telling Goldy's story for several minutes, leaving nothing out that the girl had told him about the brutal treatment she endured at Jordan's hands. "The last time he nearly killed her, and she still carries Saber's mark on her poor shoulder. That was when she conceived."

Agatha's eyes had become those of a small cornered animal.

She had difficulty looking the priest in the face. She knew with every bit of intuition she had that the story was true, but still, she wanted to deny it. "The girl's lying."

"No."

"Who is this...this creature?"

"This child is Goldy Wojna and she is standing alone except for me. No one knows about this but the three of us and, of course, Jordan.

"I won't have this...this miner's daughter bringing scandal into our home."

"Jordan has brought the scandal into your home," the old man corrected. "This girl is an innocent victim."

Agatha jumped to her feet and started to pace. "You must not let this become common knowledge. No one must know this. I have to think...."

"Something will have to be settled soon, before she starts showing."

"Yes...yes something must be done soon. Let me contact you in a couple of days. You understand, I'm not admitting anything until I talk to my son."

Agatha waited in her tower room that afternoon until she saw Jordan approaching the house. She hurried down the stairs to the back door and waited for him to come in. "I think we have something important to discuss. Please go directly to your room."

"Aw for crying out loud, Ma, I'm hungry. I'll talk to you later."

"You will go to your room and you will talk to me right *now!*"

The boy's face seemed to have a perpetual sneer anymore, Agatha observed. She followed him up the back stairs to his room, closed and locked the door.

"What's got you so upset, Ma?"

"You've got me upset, young man! Father Cassidy was here this afternoon, on behalf of the Wojna girl. He tells me that you have been misbehaving with her and that she is with child...your child. Is that true?"

Jordan went pale but still spoke with bravado. "Why would I be mixed up with Goldy Wojna? It's a lie!"

Agatha wanted to believe him, but in her heart, she felt he was lying. "You've been seen with the girl."

"So what?" He leered at her.

Something snapped in the back of Agatha's mind. Pent-up rage for all the trouble this spoiled child of hers had caused rose up in the back of her throat and almost choked her. Her face turned nearly purple just looking at his mocking manner.

She threw back her arm and struck him in the face with such a blow it almost knocked him over. He grabbed at his nose to stop the blood from rushing down the front of him, too late.

He cowered before this mother he had never known before.

"Now you will tell me the truth about this affair."

Jordan sat on the edge of his bed afraid to move. He didn't want his father called in on this, so he'd better play this one close to the vest, he thought.

"All right, all right, the little bitch seduced me and I knocked her up. What am I supposed to do about it...marry the hunky?"

"You will do exactly what I tell you to do. First of all, I forbid you to ever mention this to another living soul. Let me assure you that if you do, you will be one of the sorriest persons who ever lived. I promise you that with all my heart and soul."

Jordan believed her.

Chapter 8: Journeys

MATTHEW SAT back in the coach seat as the train rattled through a white-snow landscape. Philadelphia in the winter would be a new experience for him. He was excused for a week from school to attend what was to be a very important event in his life as an artist. Matthew did not look forward to it but felt he owed it to Arthur Cowan to be there.

Mose greeted him at the Philadelphia station. He and Gallio had formed a good friendship over the years.

"Welcome back, Mister Matthew. I've missed you."

"Thanks, Mose, but what have I told you about that Mister stuff? Matt will do fine."

Mose laughed and took the satchel from the young man's hand, placing it on the floor between them in the buggy.

"How's Mr. Cowan?"

"He's good. Very good since he heard you were coming back for a visit."

When they arrived at the house, Arthur greeted Matthew enthusiastically. "Are you ready for the big event, son?"

"No! Not ready at all."

"It isn't every day that Julian Daly accepts a new, unknown artist for a one man show in his gallery. He's very impressed with your work, Matthew."

"I'll bet I can guess who showed him my paintings." Gallio smiled a question at Arthur.

"You're wrong! It wasn't me. Well...not entirely me. Clarinda Bartholomew was your angel in this case. She showed him your painting that won the French Award and had me show him your other things here at Cowan House."

"I feel very honored."

"You should. Daly Galleries doesn't waste time or space on hacks!" The opening of your show is tomorrow night. I do have another little surprise for you. Agatha Glenn consented to loan us the portrait you painted of her for the show. It arrived yesterday. I'm sure it will be the focal point as people enter the gallery."

****

The Gallio Show opening was an understated affair by invitation only. The elite of the city's patrons and artists mixed with the socially prominent. The dress for the evening was formal, with the men in their black waistcoats, and stiff white collars. The women were swathed in chiffons and silk moire gowns in every color of the rainbow, some affecting small bustles and hoops, others wearing the newer, easier flowing look of many petticoats over tightly corseted wasp waists.

Matthew stood nervously tugging at his cravat. He was dressed in a handsome frock-coat of deep midnight blue, his white shirt crisp. He flashed his brilliant smile talking animatedly about his work to all who approached him. The small, exclusive gallery was a-buzz as people strolled and commented on the nearly forty paintings being shown for sale. The painting that seemed to impress people the most was *Agatha*. It, of course, was not for sale. From this showing, Matthew Gallio could be launched as one of the promising portrait artists to rise in the eastern United States.

Clarinda Bartholomew circulated through the crowd on Arthur's arm, a fan fluttering in her right hand. Her white hair was piled high in curls that hugged her head like a crown. Her lovely gown of periwinkle-blue chiffon rippled gracefully as she walked. She shunned hoops under her skirts but allowed for a small bustle. Approaching Matthew, her dark eyes shone. "This is your night, Matthew. We're all so proud of you."

Matt felt tongue-tied for a moment. "Thu..Thank you, ma'am. Thank you for all of your encouragement." He was still unaware that she was his patron.

"You are quite welcome. It's a pleasure to see someone's dreams come to fruition."

"By George, Matt, I knew you had it in you to be good, but this is wonderful!" Gallio felt a thump on his shoulder and turned around to see the happy face of James Peabody. The two shook hands warmly. It had been two years since they'd last met. A young girl stood close by Peabody, smiling into Gallio's eyes. *A golden girl,* Gallio thought.

Clarinda spoke up. "You remember Arienne, my granddaughter?"

"Yes, of course," he lied.

Arienne's blue eyes reminded Matthew of a blue summer sky. She couldn't have been more than fourteen, but she seemed very poised for her age. Her golden hair curled in ringlets hugging her lovely long neck that seemed to invite a kiss. The child-woman was stunning, and the young artist had difficulty pulling his eyes away from her.

"James is an old friend of the family. His father went to Englewood Academy with my son Gerald...Arienne's father." Clarinda smoothed the girl's hair with a motherly touch as she spoke.

Matthew took Arienne's small hand she offered and bent over it, wanting fervently to touch it to his lips. He released her hand quickly.

The girl, too, pressed closer to him, smiling her wonderful smile into his shining dark eyes.

He felt too warm.

The show was a success. The art critics, although careful with their praise, seemed unanimous in their opinion that Matthew Gallio had a shining future.

Only one thing marred the evening for Gallio...and that was a fleeting glimpse of a man in a waiter's uniform who he caught staring at him from behind a kiosk in the center of the gallery. Matthew could have almost sworn it was Reginald Zerby standing there with brooding eyes set upon him.

He soon forgot about the incident.

****

The news that Jordan Glenn was being sent to Natchez to Colonel Denby's Military Academy to complete his faltering education was a surprise to almost everyone in Franklinton. The ladies of the Methodist Church, which the Glenns attended, never thought that Agatha would stand for her favorite child being sent away from her for any length of time.

Agatha had been forced to tell her husband, Conrad, the truth about Jordan and his behavior toward Goldy Wojna.

Far from gnashing his teeth or pounding his desk, Conrad took a more liberal view of the whole affair, conceding only that Jordan had used poor judgment where the girl was concerned and that it was up to them, the Glenns, to make it right by the girl. To him, that meant keeping it quiet and paying her off somehow. He added that it wouldn't hurt to get her out of town. With those words, he turned his attention back to business.

So it was with foreboding that Agatha was left with the job of settling the whole problem. Jordan would be sent to military school in the south, but where could they send Goldy without anyone guessing what was going on?

A second meeting was arranged with Father Cassidy. This time Conrad Glenn sat beside his wife in their parlor when the priest arrived, his steel-gray hair combed perfectly, his round face ruddy, and his expression bored.

"We have decided that whether or not our son is truly responsible for the Wojna girl's condition, we want her spared the ridicule and scandal that would be forthcoming if her...condition became public knowledge." Conrad nodded his head automatically as Agatha talked.

"And can you tell me, Agatha, how you plan to accomplish this miracle?" The old priest was openly disturbed.

"We understand that the Wojna girl is a bright student, at the top of her class in school. Conrad and I have decided to sponsor a scholarship next month. It will also be arranged that Goldy Wojna will win that scholarship. It will also be arranged that her family will accept the opportunity their daughter is offered. A small stipend will go along with the scholarship for clothes and incidental expenses."

"What about the months before the child is born?"

"That remains a sticky problem. Tell us, Father, do you have any suggestions to make?"

"Nothing, except whatever is done, it had better be done soon."

****

Goldy, tormented and hopeless, was at that very moment making her way through hard packed snow toward Devil's Drop, a ledge that protruded high up on one of the hills. Her cheeks were red with the cold as she struggled up the last rocky slope to the ledge.

Her feet were freezing; they were almost numb, and her hands ached. They felt like ice.

When she reached the final outcropping of the ledge, she sat down for a brief moment, catching her breath. Slowly she rose and stepped off the ledge into the air.

****

"Oh my dear God!" Agatha gasped when she was told the news that Goldy Wojna had jumped from Devil's Drop. She was filled with sorrow and guilt. The guilt because she couldn't help but think the end of her problems with Goldy and the baby were settled. She was only half right.

The girl lived! The child did not. Goldy's condition was grave for weeks. Dr. Morgan made a daily visit to the Wojna shack. Agatha Glenn was also a daily visitor, bringing food and warm clothing for the girl. She would sit for hours at a time holding the unconscious girl's hand. Everyone commented on Mrs. Glenn's wonderful caring way with the young woman. Surely, few mine owners cared so much for their workers and their families. The Wojnas, Edward and Rachel, were amazed by Agatha's constant vigil.

Goldy came out of the coma on Valentine's Day. The doctor was quick to hustle everyone out of the small room Goldy occupied.

"My back hurts," the girl moaned, "and my leg has a terrible pain in it."

"I know, child. You have been through a lot. Your leg was almost shattered. But we have hopes that you will mend and walk again...perhaps with a slight limp."

Goldy nodded her head whispering, "Why didn't I die... Why didn't I die?"

"It wasn't your time to die, little girl. You must be strong and go on with your life. The child you were carrying was lost." Goldy just turned her face to the wall.

Mathew stood in front of the Wojna place, waiting to see Goldy. In his hand he held a small package, wrapped and ribboned in red for Valentine's Day.

Mrs. Wojna came to the door. "You can come in now, Matthew, but just for a few minutes. Goldy is very weak."

He walked slowly to the invalid's bed. "I...I came to give you a valentine, Goldy." He put the small package into her hand. It was no bigger than a deck of playing cards. "This is for you. I didn't need to have you there because I could see you in my mind so well." Then, gently, he kissed her pale cheek.

The girl managed a weak whisper of, "Thank you, Matthew."

Matt patted her small hand. "It's not as pretty as you really are, Goldy." He left quietly.

She seemed to be tongue-tied as one large tear slowly rolled down her cheek. Her mother opened the package for her. As she handed it to Goldy, the girl started to weep softly. The little square frame held a beautiful miniature of Goldy done in oil, her dainty face and brilliant hair shining as it used to.

****

About the middle of April, the Glenns sent for Father Cassidy to afternoon tea once again. There had been some trouble at the mine so Conrad was not present for this meeting.

"Please be seated, Father." Agatha poured tea from a silver teapot into a china cup. "Sugar?"

"No thank you."

"Conrad and I feel we should try to do something for Goldy Wojna. She will have a hard time fending for herself as a cripple. Now, mind you, this does not mean that we feel responsible for her grief...simply that we feel sorry for the girl."

"What did you have in mind?"

"We thought that perhaps we would settle three or four hundred dollars on the girl to help her along with her education, which has been so badly interrupted."

"Now let me see, Agatha. Since the baby no longer presents a threat to your reputations, you are willing to settle much less on the girl. Am I right?"

"Don't you think that's putting it rather crudely?"

"No, not crudely. Just honestly. I have counseled her from the beginning not to tell anyone about her condition. Now I must decide whether or not to counsel her to silence about why she felt she should try to take her own life."

"Are you blackmailing us, Tim Cassidy?"

"Certainly not, heaven forbid! I'm only pointing out that it might be judicious for you to send Goldy on with the original plan to enroll her in Mrs. Simon's School in Pittsburgh to complete her education and assure her some kind of future, free of scandal."

The old priest's face was earnest, and his pink skin glowed as it often did when he gambled a little.

"Of course, if you'd rather she remained in Franklinton..."

"I like your idea, Father. I'm sure Conrad will be more than pleased to offer this opportunity to one of his employees' children."

It was arranged that Goldy would leave Franklinton in September, when she should be much stronger, and start her eleventh grade in Pittsburgh with a small stipend. Upon graduation, if she excelled, she would be given five hundred dollars as a graduation gift.

Father Cassidy's round face glowed. He loved to win!

Chapter 9: Revenge

THE DALY GALLERY was in a turmoil. Word had just arrived from Franklinton, that the portrait of Agatha had been returned to the Glenn house in shreds, the canvas cut and destroyed beyond repair.

Joshua Daly was questioning all of his help. The two clerks responsible for packing the painting for its return trip to the Glenn's, sat across from him looking totally baffled.

"I'm asking you, Jim, is there any way that picture could have been vandalized like it was before it left our gallery?"

Jim Smith hesitated, thinking, then answered, "No sir. Will and I packed that picture very carefully for shipping."

Will Shuster nodded his gray head. "You know, Mr. Daly, that we are very careful with the paintings, and always have been."

"Yes, yes, I know you're both dependable, but can you think of anything different that you did in this case?"

The two helpers were silent for a minute or two, then Will said, "Our regular freight pick-up man wasn't on the wagon that night. That's the only thing different I can think of."

"Where was the regular man?"

"Don't know. Didn't think to ask."

"The man driving the wagon—what did he look like?"

"Well, I'd say he was short and dark..."

Jim nodded his head as Will spoke.

"...kind of a weasely looking type. Black hair. That's about all I can tell you, Mr. Daly."

"All I can add is that we sure are sorry this happened," Jim said, fidgeting in his chair.

"All right, all right. That'll be all. Thank you both for your help."

Arthur Cowan sat behind his desk listening to Joshua Daly's story about the stranger on the freight wagon. "It had to have happened then, and I think I know who perpetrated this vandalism."

"Who would do such a thing?"

"A bookkeeper of mine that I fired—a sworn enemy of Matthew's. I'll put out a warrant for his arrest, but I'm afraid it will be like hunting a ghost. He's very shrewd and very mean."

When Matthew heard about Agatha Glenn's portrait being destroyed, he knew almost at once who had been responsible. It was obvious to him that he had, indeed, seen Zerby at the gallery that night.

His visit to see Agatha was well received, especially when he made arrangements to do another portrait to replace the damaged one.

****

While Goldy recuperated, Jordan Glenn was packed up and sent to Dixie Military Academy in Alabama. It was not without a fight. He refused to go at first, until his father made it clear that he *would go*. His farewell from his parents and Dolly at the depot was stiff and angry all around. There were no hugs or kisses, only warnings from his father that he had better behave himself. Jordan hated warnings or threats, daring to do as he pleased. It was a somber, angry young man riding south to Alabama.

Goldy Wojna busily readied herself for her journey to Mrs. Simon's School for Young Ladies in Pittsburgh. When the departure day arrived, there was a small crowd of people waiting to send her off. Father Cassidy, Julia Keep, Matthew Gallio, Agatha Glenn, and of course, Goldy's mother and father, Rachel and Edward Wojna, who were never told about Goldy's pregnancy or the deal struck by Father Cassidy for her future. The Wojna's thought she had been awarded a scholarship for good grades.

Each person, in turn, said their goodbyes in their own way. A hug from the priest and Julia, a brief pat on the shoulder from Agatha, and many hugs and kisses from her parents.

There was a tender, gentle embrace from Matthew, the latter being the one reality she savored in her heart for a long time to come.

"Be a good girl!" her mother called as the train moved.

Goldy's face clouded only briefly.

"I'll be thinking of you often," Matthew whispered into her tiny ear.

The whistle on the engine screeched, a puff of steam blew across the platform, and Goldy was on her way. *I won't cry,* she kept telling herself, but the tears streamed down her cheeks as the group's faces disappeared into the distance.

****

Matthew started his last year of high school in September. As he walked to classes, he couldn't help but think how different this last year in school was going to be for him. His good friend Goldy was off in Pittsburgh. Even his worst enemy, Jordan Glenn, being absent would leave a slightly empty feeling in his thoughts.

By Christmas, Matthew felt the year rushing by. He received his stipend from his still-unknown benefactress along with a nice Christmas present of fifty dollars. About once a month he received a note from Goldy, which told him very little except that she was well and working hard at school. Other than that, it had become a bit hum-drum for him in Franklinton, and he was looking forward to graduation and his return to Philadelphia.

His almost daily visits to Glenn House were the one bright spot in his existence.

"Do you think this new portrait will be as good as the first?" Agatha sounded a bit anxious. Secretly, she, too, looked forward to sitting in the afternoons in her parlor. They opened all the draperies and let in as much light as possible. It also helped her to stop brooding over Jordan's departure.

Matthew didn't tell her that he could detect a deep sorrow in her eyes that he had never seen before. Neither did he mention her son's absence.

The letter from Arthur Cowan was in his Christmas card to Matthew, written in Cowan's back-slanted, dark-black script:

Dear Matthew,

I have heard from Agatha Glenn that you are doing her portrait again. It pleases me that you are so conscientious and dependable. However, I want you to know that Zerby seems to be the vandal. Apparently he is still holding a grudge against you. Please be alert when you travel to Philadelphia again...take care. I don't believe you have to worry in Franklinton—I hope.

Your friend,
Arthur Cowan

Matthew felt a cold chill after he read the note. There was nothing he could do to protect himself. As always he took the problem to Father Cassidy. Although Gallio felt better after his talk with the priest and offering his prayers, he still dreaded another encounter with Zerby. With time, he hoped to push all thoughts of the man out of his mind.

While Matthew was finishing the details on Agatha's portrait, she asked him if he would also paint Dolly for her sixteenth birthday. What he didn't know was that Dolly had requested the portrait by Gallio.

Dolly was tall like her mother. There the resemblance ended. Her fine white porcelain-like skin was unblemished, her hair a true rose-gold. Slender and graceful, she had a bit of the gamin about her, a charming tomboy. Although Matthew had not yet ventured into painting nudes, he couldn't help speculating about what a beautiful nude she would make. He looked at his feet and tried pushing those thoughts from his mind. He hoped to God no one noticed his appraising eyes running over her body.

She had not yet started to sit for him. "What shall I wear?" Dolly asked him pointedly.

"Well...uh...something green, I think." He blushed furiously.

"Light green or dark green?" Dolly pressed him.

"Either should work for you," he said, fidgeting with his paint box.

"And should my hair be up or let down?" Dolly's eyes twinkled as she detected his discomfort.

I wish this damn girl would get out of here, he thought. Questions and more questions.

The girl sat down in a brocaded side-chair, placing both of her small hands under her strong chin, elbows on knees, heart-shaped face eagerly awaiting an answer to her last question.

"Down," Matthew choked. Then finding his composure... "By all means, down." He walked out of the parlor and left the house.

Dolly watched him leave, wondering what she'd done to upset him.

The second portrait of Agatha was completed and hung in the parlor over the mantel. True to his word, it was even more compelling than the first.

He started with Dolly's sittings immediately. Every afternoon except Saturdays and Sundays, he sat painting for an hour or more while the girl fidgeted.

At first Matthew found her silly and difficult to talk to. After a few afternoons, she started asking him intelligent questions about his work, which impressed him. He had no way of knowing that she had hidden several volumes on portrait painting under her bed, which she had accumulated from the county library. Dolly poured over them nightly.

One day when she felt particularly devilish, she said, "You don't like me, do you?"

Matthew's eyes widened. He looked surprised. "Why do you say such a thing?"

"There you go, evading the question."

"That isn't true. Of course I like you; we're old friends from school."

"I wouldn't say we're old friends. Really, we hardly know each other." Dolly pouted.

"All right then, we're not old friends, we're acquaintances. Does that make you feel better?" He was getting irritated with her.

"No. And you still haven't answered my question."

"All right, I like you fine." His face was very red. "Let's hang it up for today." It was a statement not a question.

There was little Dolly could think of to say. She certainly had been dismissed, so she left the parlor, her own face scarlet.

While Matthew cleaned his brushes, he pondered on the complex personality of Dolly Glenn. She certainly wasn't like any of the other girls he knew at school. A mystery to him.

Dolly Glenn's portrait was, perhaps, the best piece of work Gallio had ever done. The heart-shaped face with its moist, pouting lips, wide-set green eyes (so full of secrets) staring soulfully from the canvas, stopped the viewers in their tracks.

Few people even noticed the lime-colored chiffon dress that trailed off from a tiny bouffant bustle in the back, accenting the perfect figure that was only hinted at. Matthew tried to cover her rich curves with soft chiffon folds. The full-length portrait was almost exotic, with the girl's light copper-colored curls cascading over a slightly exposed, firm left breast.

How many times he had yearned to touch that breast as she sat before him in her teasing way. These feelings he examined for himself and decided that he must resist such thoughts of the flesh, especially Dolly Glenn's flesh!

Chapter 10: Surprises

IT WAS MARCH when the black-dragon of a train steamed into Franklinton. Its flatcars were laden with lumber, barrels of nails and screws, but the most exciting sight for the townspeople was the carriage that was strapped down on the middle car. It was grand by all standards of the word. A landau, painted blue and white, with lovely blue horsehair upholstery. It seated six passengers, three facing each other on each side with a driver's seat up front.

The townspeople were gathering on the platform at the depot, each one anxious to have a look at the carriage and perhaps its owner. Even the Glenn's carriage was not as sumptuous as the one on the train.

Fred Slager, the bank president, stood back away from the crowd fingering his gold watch chain and smiling to himself. A man dressed in a fine frock coat and beaver felt bowler stepped down from the passenger car onto the platform. He approached Slager. "I assume you are Mr. Slager, my correspondent?"

Fred, hatless, extended his pudgy hand to the well attired Gerald Bartholomew, shaking the man's hand firmly. Bartholomew stood a head taller than the banker.

"Ah, Mr. Bartholomew, prompt as always I see."

"I don't believe in wasting time."

"Then let's go over to my office at once. I believe I have all the papers ready for your signature."

"Presently. Please wait a few minutes for my mother to leave the train. She hates traveling...says it upsets her equilibrium."

At that moment, there was a whispering among the people watching as Clarinda Bartholomew stepped down from the parlor car. Her silver hair reflected the sun, making it look like a halo. Her traveling suit was raspberry wool, beautifully tailored to fit her perfectly. A tiny hat, matching the suit, dangled from her gloved hand, and over one arm she carried a soft beaver coat.

Old Slager caught his breath, thinking her beautiful. The curious crowd seemed to agree, but Clarinda swept by them as if they were invisible. "My dear man," she addressed Slager, "that was one hell of a train ride up that mountain. I'm glad I won't have to make the trip often." Then she laughed her wonderful, musical laugh, completely disarming Fred. The men were fussing and helping her into the waiting buggy Fred had brought. Poor Slager was totally smitten.

As the buggy rolled through the streets of the town, Fred pointed out the places of interest.

"Show me where the land that I bought is located," Clarinda requested. The buggy stopped.

"See that high shelf near the top of Bear Mountain?" He pointed his finger toward the spot.

"That's Queen's Rest. Your ten acres are up there, right off the Coalport Trail."

Clarinda shaded her eyes with one hand. "Beautiful! What's the meaning of the name?"

"It seems an old Shawnee Indian chief married a young Indian maiden against her wishes. She was in love with a young warrior. While the chief was absent on a hunting party, she climbed Bear Mountain trying to escape. When she reached that spot there," Slager pointed again, "she was caught, so she ate some hemlock and lay down and died."

"Well, the poor soul!" Clarinda was silent a while, then she said, "I'm going to call my house Queen's Escape." Gerald rolled his eyes and coughed.

The three arrived at the bank, going straight to Fred's desk. All the papers were signed, naming Clarinda Bartholomew sole owner of the acreage they had discussed.

"We're prepared to start the lodge right away," Gerald told Fred. Can you tell us where we can stay for a few days as I get the work crew started? I'd like for my men to be accommodated, too, while they build the lodge for Mother."

"I've arranged for everything." Fred beamed and rubbed his hands together. "My sister lives with me, and you will be most welcome in our home while you are here. The workmen you brought are to live at Hickman's boarding house until the lodge is built. I hope that is all right?"

"My English Shires...my horses...will need special attention, Mr. Slager." Clarinda smiled. "They are very valuable you know...."

"Our livery stable is excellent and will take very good care of your horses."

"I am impressed." Clarinda offered her hand.

Fred was so pleased he could barely speak.

With the Bartholomews settled into the home of Fred and Emma Slager, the townspeople settled down to a steady buzz about the great lodge being built up the mountain; there had never been anything around Franklinton quite like it.

Matthew was not unaware of the rich visitors in town and remembered he had met the great lady everyone talked about. He chose, however, to keep his distance, fearing Clarinda would not remember him, and he didn't want to appear pushy.

His fears were unfounded, as he discovered the second day they were in town.

While hurrying to the Glenn house to meet Dolly for a sitting, the magnificent landau rolled by. He saw Clarinda seated in the back staring at him. He quickly waved and flashed his wonderful smile.

Poking the driver with her parasol, she ordered him to stop, then motioned Matthew to come to her.

"What a rich surprise! My favorite artist right here in Franklinton! How are you, Gallio?"

"I'm fine, Mrs. Bartholomew"...then remembering his manners, "How are you?"

"Now that I've met someone I actually know in this town, I'm a lot better. Makes me less homesick for Philadelphia."

"I think I can understand what you mean. When I left home that first summer to study with Mr. Cowan, I thought I'd never get used to that place, but I did."

"Arthur can put you at ease all right. Now tell me, what are you doing? Are you working on anything right at the moment?"

"Well besides going to school, I'm doing a portrait of Dolly Glenn, Mrs. Glenn's daughter," he said, tilting his head toward the Glenn house.

"My! How I'd like to see it. May I see it, Matthew?"

"I don't know...uh... I'd have to get Mrs. Glenn's approval for that."

"Fine." She poked the driver with her parasol again to get him going. "You let me know when it's convenient, Matthew." The carriage rolled on.

Why is it, thought Gallio, *that it seems to be settled already?*

****

Gerald spent his days at the work site dressed in rough corduroy trousers and high boots that came up to his knees.

He kept a woolen plaid over-shirt over his fine linen. A battered, broad-rimmed felt hat was slouched on his head, covering most of his gray hair. Every night those boots had to be cleaned of the daily accumulation of mud, and his woolen shirt brushed clean. Of course that fell to the Slagers' maid, who was none too happy about the whole arrangement.

Clarinda laughed when she saw her son in his "work clothes," as he called them. "Looks more like cowboy attire to me," she chuckled.

Secretly, the comparison pleased Gerald very much, since he had a romance with the American West.

Of course Agatha Glenn was only too eager to have Mrs. Bartholomew make her a visit. *Only right,* she thought. It was arranged for the day after the request.

Clarinda arrived at Agatha's door promptly at three o'clock in the afternoon. Matthew escorted her to the door, staying only long enough to make the introductions. He quickly disappeared from sight.

The visitor was wearing a flowered afternoon dress of wool crepe that boasted many rich embroidered colors and a very tiny bustle. The soft wool capelet over her shoulders was piped in the same material as the dress. Grosgrain ribbon held it in place. Her small pillbox hat (very new in those climes) was covered with multicolored feathers.

If Agatha felt outdone, she certainly didn't show it. She greeted Clarinda serenely, showing her into the tastefully furnished parlor. Her own dress, in stark contrast to her guest's, was a fitted light brown wool crepe with matching satin-covered buttons running to the waist. Satin trimmed the high neckline that was accented with a magnificent cameo brooch. The long fitted sleeves had slashed puffs at the elbows that were lined with a contrasting colored satin. No bustle was evident, just a slight gathering in the back to suggest a gentle flow. She looked elegant.

Tea was served by the maid, and talk about the lodge being built monopolized the conversation for some time until Clarinda eyed the new portrait of Agatha over the mantel.

"My dear Mrs. Glenn, what a wonderful likeness of you! But it isn't the portrait I remember seeing at the Daly Gallery.

"No, it isn't. I had no idea you had seen the first."

"Indeed, I did see it and thought it was striking."

Agatha tried not to show her pleasure. "The first was destroyed by a vandal before it was shipped back to us. Matthew was kind enough to have me sit again for this one."

"I thought the original was his finest work so far, but now I must say this one is even better!" Their friendship seemed to be off to a flying start.

Matthew showed up at that moment from behind the screens at the end of the parlor where the portrait of Dolly was being done.

"I would be very honored to show you both the portrait of Miss Glenn that is in progress. Of course it is not yet completed, but it will be soon." He was very nervous as he stood aside for the two women to walk closer toward the life-sized canvas.

An intake of breath was heard in the room. He wasn't sure which woman had made the sound.

Clarinda spoke first. "This is wonderful, Matthew, just exquisite." Her face glowed.

"Yes, yes," Agatha agreed. "It is wonderful."

Matthew's face was damp with nervous perspiration. His pleasure at the compliments also showed on his face. Every emotion ran through his body...relief, embarrassment, surprise, and pride...yes, even pride, which surprised him.

"Thank you," was all he managed to say to the two women.

The women had left and Gallio was busy pulling the screens over in front of the painting again. He bent over his paint box, making sure he was prepared for the sitting the next day when he heard a creaking of the floorboards behind him.

Dolly was standing by the parlor doors, which she slid firmly closed and locked. Her moist mouth was slightly open and she had a faint smile moving on her face.

"Why Dolly, we haven't got a sitting until tomorrow afternoon!"

"Yes, I know." She started unbuttoning her white blouse which she'd worn to school.

Matthew was silent for a moment, not really gathering what was happening.

Next she freed herself from the school-girl skirt and let it drop to the floor. Her shining eyes never left Matthew's face, who was by that time blushing furiously. He wanted to quit looking at her, but he found he couldn't.

"How many times have you wanted to undress me?" Dolly stood there in her undergarments. "Answer me, dammit."

Matthew felt strangled and short of breath. She had seen his lust behind his eyes.

Standing there in the glow of the late afternoon sun, she seemed to be glowing with desire, as she dropped her petticoats and then pulled down the straps of her chemise.

"You...you mustn't do this, Dolly. This isn't right."

"It's right for me. I've been waiting and waiting for you to touch me."

"Now, Dolly, you're just a child."

"I'm sixteen, and I know what I want." She sat down on the chair she was being painted in and removed her shoes and hose.

Matthew was frantically moving around the parlor picking up her clothing where she had dropped them, and after he had them all in his arms, he stood before her, holding them like an offering to the gods. "Please, Dolly, get dressed!"

Instead, she stood up and pressed her naked body against him, laughing. "I can tell you don't really want me to...not really," and she ran her hands down his thighs.

Anger welled up in Gallio's chest. Anger at the girl for discovering his lust, anger at himself for his body responding in spite of himself. His mouth came down hard on those moist lips he had coveted and lingered over so long. His tongue parted her mouth and she responded with her own tongue.

Nothing could have stopped him then; it was hopeless—except for Agatha's voice on the other side of the locked parlor door. "Dolly, are you in there?"

The girl grabbed her clothing from the floor and squeezed through one of the long parlor windows, escaping into the bushes, leaving Matthew to explain the locked door and his late presence in the house.

He hurried to the door. "I'm sorry, Mrs. Glenn, I didn't realize the door was locked. I closed it so I wouldn't disturb you moving the screens back in place." He hoped she would not notice the stocking hanging from the end of his easel. He grabbed it, wadded it into a ball, and proceeded to wipe a brush on it, as if cleaning the brush.

"Have you seen Dolly?"

"Yes, she went by the window a while back and waved to me."

That girl...I can never find her when I want her. I'll see you tomorrow, Matthew." Agatha bustled away.

Matthew left the house quickly, promising himself never to allow Dolly to entice him again. One thing bothered the young man about the whole incident, and that was how Dolly Glenn had learned her sophisticated ways. He would have to go to confession this week, for sure.

Chapter 11: Maturity

IT WAS TWO or three weeks before the townspeople settled back into their everyday routines. The Bartholomews had returned to Philadelphia and everyone was getting used to the workmen from the lodge spending lively weekends at Keller's Saloon. The big new house that was being built up the mountain was only a mild curiosity anymore.

Dolly's portrait had been finished by Matthew, and he had managed to avoid further entanglements with Dolly, who pouted every time she saw the artist. The painting was a smashing success and caused much speculation in town as to whether or not Dolly Glenn really was that exotic looking.

Agatha hung the portrait in the large entrance hall of Glenn House, where it was the first thing the eye fell upon when entering. She was very happy with the likeness, giving Gallio a nice bonus when it was done. As for Dolly's opinion, she ignored it, seeming to deny its very presence in the house. She refused to discuss the painting at all. Very perplexing for Agatha.

Letters had been few in number from Jordan. When Agatha did receive one, she would hurry to her special retreat at the top of the house to be alone while she read it. They were all alike— hateful accusations for his parents because of where they had sent him, and complaints about everything at the academy. Always there was the request for money.

Conrad Glenn finally stopped reading them, telling Agatha, "You handle it."

Jordan wrote one letter accusing Colonel Denby of physically abusing him, saying, "I didn't do anything. One of the other cadets lied to get out of punishment."

This was too much for Agatha; her habitual response of sheltering her son was evident again. She wrote a scathing letter to the Colonel asking for an explanation. The answer arrived quickly.

DIXIE MILITARY ACADEMY
April 2, 1958
Dear Madam:

It is with regret that I must inform you of the conduct of your son. It is our policy to try and settle behavior problems ourselves. However, since Jordan has chosen to involve his parents in this, I have no choice but to inform you what has transpired.

As you know, the young men share rooms. Jordan was given Cadet Jacobs as his roommate.

Cadet Jacobs may be credited with saving Jordan's life. It seems your son had cut through the floor boards in their room to make a hidey-hole to hold a rather large cache of liquor under the floor boards.

Last month, on a given evening, your son partook of large quantities of liquor to the point of unconsciousness. Although Cadet Jacobs feared reporting on Jordan, he feared for Jordan's life more and reported the situation to me.

Jordan has refused to follow the honor system here at DIXIE. His academic endeavors have been almost nonexistent, which brings me to another painful revelation. Jordan will not graduate with his class this year.

If a decision is made by you, his parents, to send him to us to complete his senior year (next year), we would require assurances from you that his performance would be serious. Otherwise, he will not be accepted again at DIXIE.

We are living in serious political times and hope our cadets will be worthy of any challenge that we might be called upon to answer.

It is with deep regret that we feel it necessary to write this communication to you and we will await your answer.

COLONEL MARSHALL J. DENBY, ADJUTANT, DIXIE MILITARY ACADEMY

The Glenns faced each other over the long mahogany dinner table, long since cleared by Millie.

Dolly had been excused from the table. The silence between the two was exacerbated by the steady, echoing tick of the grandfather clock in the entry hall.

Agatha's head was beating with a headache. She looked strained and weak.

Conrad sat, head down, as if he'd been beaten and had no recourse. He finally broke the silence. "What are we to do?"

"Not this time, Conrad. Not this time! My decisions made alone have not solved anything. This time you are going to be involved in our son's future. Not me alone."

"The children and the house I have left up to you. I thought you wanted it that way. Anyhow, you know the mines demand a lot of my attention." Hearing himself, he felt justified in his attitude.

"That's all I hear from you is 'the mines, the mines.' Has it ever occurred to you that Jordan might have needed his father's attention?" Her eyes, red rimmed, were angry.

"Yes, Agatha, it occurred to me, but you were always there standing between us...afraid Jordan would be punished or hurt. You can't blame this on me. Now...what are WE going to do?"

She started to sob.

"Now listen to me." Conrad brought his fist down on the table lightly. "We'll allow the Colonel to mete out whatever punishment he deems necessary, then Jordan will finish this year there. Since he has ruined his reputation at the school already, there is little to be accomplished by sending him back next year. We'll consider other options for next year. I'm sure my brother in Texas will be willing to take him for rough work on his spread for the coming summer. Do you agree?"

"Yes, Conrad," Agatha answered meekly.

Jordan's immediate future seemed settled.

Chapter 12: Encounters

GOLDY LIKED PITTSBURGH and was doing well at Miss Simon's School. She had her sixteenth birthday on April seventh of her first year at the school.

Her wardrobe, which Agatha had chosen for her, held her in good stead with the other girls. She was dressed conservatively. Leaning toward frugality, she managed to save part of the monthly allowance the Glenns provided for her; in fact, she had a nice little nest egg put into the bank by the end of the first year. It gave her great pleasure to walk into the First Federal Bank of Pittsburgh and plunk down her five or ten dollars each month.

It was during one of her visits to the bank that she first met James Peabody. James was home from Princeton for spring break and running some errands for his father. He first noticed her shining red hair, which had returned to its glowing hue. The green dress she wore accented her tiny waist and made her large azure eyes look even more blue.

James could not keep his eyes away from her. His black frock coat and high hat made him appear older than his nineteen years. When Goldy dropped her deposit book, it was James who hurriedly retrieved it for her.

Bowing slightly, he introduced himself. "My name is James Peabody." No stutter remained.

Goldy looked frightened and took a step backward. "How do you do." She did not offer her hand but moved away quickly toward the door where another girl seemed to be waiting for her. They both left the bank and entered a waiting carriage. As she stepped into the carriage, James noticed her slight limp.

He stood motionless watching the carriage roll away, certain that he had just seen the most beautiful girl in the world.

"Do you know that young woman who just made a deposit?" He leaned over the counter toward the teller who had taken care of Goldy's business.

"Sorry, Mr. Peabody; all I know is she comes in about once a month to make a deposit."

"Can you tell me her name?"

"You should know that's against the rules." The girl twinkled a dimple back at him.

It finally cost him an expensive dinner at the Grand Hotel and a small gold brooch before he got Goldy's name and address.

The roses arrived at Miss Simon's, addressed to Goldy, on April tenth. She was overwhelmed with the flowers. Miss Simons sniffed her disapproval when she handed them to the girl. "What have you done to deserve these?" She sniffed again through her skinny, aquiline nose.

"Why...why nothing, Miss Simons, Ma'am. I have only met the young man once."

"Humph...and where was that?"

"At the bank, last week."

"Remember, we do not tolerate suitors for our students. Especially those who are only fifteen." Her finger wobbled in front of Goldy's nose.

"But, Miss Simons, I'm sixteen now!"

"No matter...no matter; there will be no suitors allowed until you are a senior. And then, only by permission of your parents."

"Yes Ma'am." Goldy lowered her head and smiled behind the roses. She hadn't been so happy since Matthew hugged her and kissed her cheek at the railroad station.

Goldy's roommate, Jenny DeWitt, made appreciative sounds and inhaled the lovely aroma of the roses. "Tell me Goldy, who sent you such an offering?"

"Just a young man I met at the bank last week. I really don't know anything about him except he said his name is James Peabody."

"Not THE James Peabody?" Jenny jumped up and down clapping her hands.

"Well, I don't know if he's THE James Peabody or not, but he wears gold rimmed glasses and is quite blond."

"That's him...that's him! Don't you know that his father is one of the richest men in Pittsburgh? He has his financial finger in many pies."

"That's nice." Goldy seemed unimpressed.

"He's one of the most eligible young men around here."

Goldy started to laugh. "I guess that leaves me out, because according to Miss Simons, I won't be eligible myself for another year or so."

"You are so lucky to have caught his eye and yet you stand there, cleaning out your dresser drawer as if nothing has happened."

"Nothing has." And that seemed to be the end of the conversation for Goldy.

It was several weeks before James was heard from again. It was a warm, late May afternoon, and Jenny and Goldy were taking a stroll around the block before dinner. A beautiful, two-wheeled carriage, pulled by two black horses approached the girls. It stopped beside them. "Can you direct me to the school with the most beautiful girls in Pittsburgh?" They all laughed.

James Peabody had found his quarry.

After that, it was easy for James to find Goldy and her roommate walking before dinner, but he wanted to talk to Goldy alone.

The first note he wrote was simple and to the point:

> *Dear Goldy:*
> *Where can we meet alone?*
> *I must talk to you.*
> *JP*

The next time the group met, Goldy handed him her answer.

It is strictly forbidden until I am a senior.
Just finishing my sophomore year. Sorry.
GW

The passing of notes was firmly established between the two. Just as they found ways to pass notes back and forth they started to correspond regularly when James went back to school.

He was totally smitten with the miner's daughter.

They wrote about many things, even the poverty from which Goldy had come. To James it made no difference; he loved this bright, beautiful girl.

With the discovery that Goldy came from Franklinton, James was delighted to learn that his friend Matthew and Goldy were lifelong friends. Goldy was careful not to reveal her passionate feelings for Gallio.

The growing pleasure that she felt in the company of James was marred only by her secret adoration of Matthew.

It was arranged that Goldy Wojna would spend her summer sojourn from school at the home of Miss Simon's sister, Mrs. Tyler, who had three young children. After a quick trip home to Franklinton to visit briefly with her parents, she was off to the Catskill Mountains to act as a summer nanny for the Tyler children.

Goldy's goodbyes to James were unemotional for her, but quietly tormenting for James, who wasn't quite sure how he could get along without seeing her for three and a half months.

Although Goldy longed to see Matthew while she was home, she was greatly relieved to find that he had already departed for Philadelphia for the summer classes. Her trip to the Catskills was made easier knowing Matthew was not around.

An urgent message in August informed Matthew that Father Cassidy was ill. He hurriedly packed his things, and after saying his goodbyes, Mose took him to the railroad station.

He was met by Fred Slager at the Franklinton station.

"Glad you're home, Matthew." He held out his big ham of a hand. "Father Timothy has been going downhill for several weeks. Julia has been fussing that you should come back to the parsonage." Fred was a little surprised at the size of the young man. He was certainly taller than his father had been. *He must be six feet tall,* he thought. But he favored his mother's northern Italian looks. Light complexioned with blue eyes. He did, however, have the black curly hair of his father. Looking at him, Fred decided that he was a young man set on where he was going, with few obstacles that would change his course. He had not filled out yet, but one day he would be a powerfully built man. Fred could see that.

Julia was at the parsonage door, wiping her hands on her apron as she greeted Matthew. "Oh, Matthew, I have prayed that you'd come home to us soon."

"I got here as fast as I could. What seems to be troubling Father Timothy?"

"We ain't sure, but he gets weaker every week, and now he is refusing to eat as he should. He just seems weary all the time, and you know things are bad with him when he cannot hold mass."

Familiar smells wafted into the hallway from the kitchen. Chicken soup was in the air and Matthew felt sure there would be dumplings to go with it. "Julia, is that your famous chicken soup I smell? I always miss your wonderful cooking." He headed for the kitchen where he had always hung his cloak. "Can I see Father now?"

Fred had followed him into the kitchen, "I think that would be the best medicine he could get."

Julia agreed. "Come on, I'll go up with you. I want to see his face when he sees you're here."

The three good friends climbed the stairs to Father Timothy's bedroom. The old priest lay plumped up on a mountain of white pillows, his round face not quite as full as it had been, but his eyes sparkled nevertheless when he saw Matthew come through the door. After some brief conversation among them, Julia and Fred left Father Timothy and Matthew alone together.

"Is there anything I can do for you, sir?" Matthew hardly knew what to say, for he had always depended on the priest's strength during the years, and suddenly he was the strong one himself.

"I'm just delighted that you got here, Matthew. Yes there is something you can do for me. I want you to go over to my dresser and pull the third drawer out. In the back, there is a wooden box. I'd like for you to bring that to me."

Gallio found the box where it was supposed to be and took it across the room to the priest. He laid it on the bed beside him. The old man fingered the catch and it came open. Reaching into the box, his hands shaking, he took out a packet of papers wrapped with string. "Come sit close to the bed, son."

Matthew pulled the side chair close to the bed.

"These are the things that must be taken care of when I go.

"Oh, Father, please don't talk like that. Haven't you always told me there is always hope in Christ?"

"I understand, but there is a time for everyone, and my time has come." The old man's body was wracked with coughing, and he covered his mouth with a handkerchief to cover the blood that came out. "These papers dispose of my worldly belongings as I planned. I've managed to save a small nest egg to take care of any debts I might be leaving and any funeral expenses the church does not cover. Then I have left a remembrance to Julia, who has always been so faithful. The remaining money, which is not a lot but should keep you frugally for some time, is yours."

"Father, please don't worry about me, surely there is some family that will want to claim your estate."

"There is no one left of my people, and you are the same as a son to me." He patted Matthew's hand, which lay on the coverlet.

It was time for Matthew Gallio to remember that any strength he had must be shown to his guardian so that he would not worry about his survival. He tried to hold back tears, which stubbornly crowded the corners of his eyelids.

Julia tapped lightly on the door. "Mr. Matthew, could I see you outside, for a moment?" He followed her quietly into the hall. "Father Jeffrey, the new pastor, just arrived.

He and Father Timothy have worked together in the past. He wants to be with Father Timothy now." Matthew understood at once and nearly collapsed against the wall in the hall.

"Please ask him if he can wait a moment longer. I must say something important to Father." With that, he reentered the priest's bedroom and approached the bed. Taking the frail hand of the old man in his hand, he knelt close to his ear and murmured, "I love you, my dear father, do you hear me?" The priest's eyes brightened for a moment then seemed to fade again. Matthew blindly stumbled from the room.

It was decided by Father Jeffrey and Gallio that the young man would continue to use his familiar room at the parsonage until he had settled for a place of his own. Julia was delighted with the arrangement for she had come to consider Gallio as family.

The grieving time for Matthew was hard and lonely. He started to take long hikes into the woods and up the mountain paths. He was not yet ready to return to the school in Philadelphia.

It was on one of these hikes that Matthew found the tiny bubbling creek just below the new Bartholomew lodge. It became a special place for him to stop and spend time just thinking. The quiet little stream was as clear as crystal, bubbling over rocks and fallen twigs. He did not know that Clarinda Bartholomew and her granddaughter, Arienne, were already spending some late summer time at the lodge before it was completely finished. Clarinda had wanted to be present to oversee the landscaping and the stone porches so they would be what she specified.

One day as he lay back gazing up at the blue late summer sky, he saw her standing on the edge of a rise just above the creek. Arienne was wearing an ankle length white dress trimmed with smocking across the top, and a wide blue satin ribbon flowed down the back of a softly draped, bustle-like puff at the back. She was without a bonnet and the parasol she was supposed to be carrying was tossed aside.

She stood in the sunlight, gazing around. *A golden girl,* Matthew thought. He was startled by her beauty.

She turned then and saw him. "I see you down there," her lilting voice called out. Her smile dazzled him. It took Matthew a few minutes to realize who she was. *Of course,* he thought, *the Bartholomew girl.* Something stopped him from approaching her, but nothing seemed to stand in her way, as she came scrambling down the grade to the creek. "Are you rude, or does the cat have your tongue?"

Gallio just laughed at that. This was not to be a girl to ignore...anyway, how could he ignore her?

"I'm sorry. I'm afraid you just surprised me."

"My name is Arienne. What's yours?" So petite, she had to look up at his face. Golden curls covered her head.

"I'm Matthew Gallio. I must say you have changed a lot since we first met. You were mud all over at that first meeting."

Arienne looked at him quizzically, not understanding what he was referring to. "Where was that?"

"That was a long time ago in Mr. Cowan's parlor."

Arienne blushed pink but not for long. "That was not a gentlemanly thing to say to a lady." Then she appraised him with her cornflower-blue eyes for a minute before she started to giggle. "I was a mess. I remember!" Then they both laughed.

Without an invitation, she settled herself down on a log very close to Matthew. Conversation came easily between the two, and Arienne sat quietly speaking and in turn listening while she reached out, touching the cold water and feeling it run through her fingers.

It became a habit, their meeting at the creek each sunny afternoon. Matthew started to bring his sketching pad and spent time drawing various head poses of the girl as they talked or walked near the stream. He always thought of her as his golden girl, although he never spoke of it to her.

They had been meeting for a couple of weeks when trouble entered the scene. Arienne had just left him one afternoon when Gallio headed down the mountain back to town. He hadn't gone more than one hundred yards when he was tackled to the ground by a huge, rough looking man with a piece of chain. Matthew had never seen him before. After knocking Matthew to the ground, the giant-of-a-man sat on his stomach and pounded his head into the ground. Gallio managed to roll over and right himself just long enough to run a few yards. The giant caught up with him and pulling at his right arm, twisted it so roughly that Matthew thought he was going to tear it off. The pain was excruciating, and just as the attack seemed to be over, Matthew heard a familiar voice order, "Here, finish him off with this." Gallio could just see another figure, smaller and dark, hand his tormentor a club-like piece of log. His mind barely working, he still knew who it was...Zerby. He remembered nothing after that.

Chapter 13: Salvation

THE MASSIVE OAK DOOR to the bedroom Matthew occupied seemed to be constantly opening and closing. The shades in the room that covered the huge windows overlooking the mountains were pulled to a halfway position, allowing enough light in to lift the dreariness and shutting off enough light to keep Matthew's eyes from being bothered. The bed he lay in was large enough for three people, at least, standing near a window giving a good view of an outside porch on the second floor.

The maid and butler were busy seeing to the invalid's needs. Clarinda worried in and out at least five times a day, while Arienne almost camped outside the door, perched in a large tapestry chair with wooden arms and fat wooden legs.

The patient was suffering from a broken left arm, broken ribs, which the doctor taped so heavily he looked almost like a mummy, and he had a head concussion. He had not awakened for a whole day. Dr. Young, the town doctor, had predicted Matthew would return to consciousness at any moment. He reported that with proper care, within the next few weeks, he would survive the beating.

With Clarinda policing his nursing care, it was obvious that the best of care would be exactly what he was going to get. She questioned and pestered the poor doctor so much that he was delighted to crawl into his buggy each day to leave the Queen's Escape.

It was the evening of the second day after the assault on Matthew that Arienne snuggled in the chair in the hall as usual. She heard a quiet moan emanate from the room. Swiftly, she pushed the heavy door open then ran to the bedside of the patient.

Gallio's head, bandaged and still bloody, was tilted toward her. His eyes, both swollen, black and blue, were just slits. He moved and whimpered something. Arienne put her cool hand to his forehead, whispering assurances to him, which he seemed to understand for he relaxed a little. "I'm right here, Matthew. You're going to be all right, really you are. We won't let anything happen to you." Her voice, like a kiss.

Matthew went to sleep then and was quiet the rest of the night. The girl stayed by his side until her grandmother made her go to bed.

Clarinda sent for Father Jeffrey the next day. It was decided between them that Matthew would stay with the Bartholomews for the remainder of his long convalescence.

Arienne was ecstatic, but she hid it very well.

It was a couple of weeks before Matthew was able to feed himself, so the job fell to the maid. However, she was relieved of that chore by Arienne at least two or three times a day.

Matthew's first conscious memories after the beating were of the golden girl patiently spooning soup and soft foods into his mouth. At first it was such an effort for him to swallow that he dreaded meal times, but slowly he began to look forward to seeing the girl sitting on his bed, leaning over him with the spoon, spooning in his food.

The one blessing was that his hands had not been injured. They were stiff and puffy, but each day they looked more normal.

Although Matthew was able to identify the culprits who had accosted him, there were no signs of the thugs. Gallio wondered if that would be the last time Zerby would try for the revenge he seemed set on visiting upon him. The young artist did not understand how Zerby could hold such a grudge against him when he, in fact, had done nothing to the man. It was all imagined in the mind of the ex-bookkeeper.

Arienne started to bring books to Matthew's bed, where she would spend many hours reading to him. Sometimes it was poetry from Longfellow, or even Whittier, which she found less romantic. Her patient didn't care what she read. Just the lilting sound of her lovely voice was enough for him to be satisfied.

It became a habit that he would hold her hand as she sat by his bed. She responded by leaning ever closer to him, as if seeking a heat that she needed to warm herself. If he didn't reach for her hand, she would lift his hand, placing it on top of hers.

It was soon obvious to all who entered the room that the two were living in their own world. It was a world no one else could enter. As soon as Matthew could walk by himself, he used his cane to help him walk down to the brook where they had met. The leaves were changing into the jeweled hues of fall. Arienne always followed him when she thought no one was watching.

The two would embrace as soon as they were out of sight of the house. Breathlessly they clutched each other, desire burning in their hearts until it was almost impossible to not fulfill the inevitable feelings they had for each other. A soft kiss turned into an exchange of tongues touching, and Matthew tried to resist discovering her body with his hands, clasping her small breasts, kissing them through the cloth of her dress. It left Arienne breathless, but it was not enough for her...she needed him.

They walked toward the stables behind the lodge, where they discovered a storage shed in the rear, only half finished.

It was always deserted for the workers were busy on the front of the lodge. It was there that the lovers found a place to be alone together. Arienne would come to him after leaving her undergarments in her room. There was no more fumbling for intimacy between them. He could free her breasts and press his mouth against their lovely pale skin, the pink nubbins of her breasts standing erect for him.

"We shouldn't..." Matthew choked.

"Don't stop. Don't ever stop...I need you for every minute of my life, my darling."

Matthew lay down as close to Arienne as he could, stroking her thighs and between her legs where she was already wet, ready for him. He felt her hand take hold of him as he throbbed for her.

"Do it...do it," she begged, guiding him into her own golden mound with throaty, soft encouraging words. Their explosion came at the same moment rocking them both into another world.

"My darling, there will never be anyone else for me," Matthew whispered into her ear.

"Never for me, Matthew,...never. I love you so."

****

Gerald Bartholomew arrived in early October to help Clarinda and Arienne prepare for their trip back to Philadelphia for the winter season.

Clarinda spoke to her son as soon as possible about the obvious attraction that had taken place while Gallio was staying in the house. "This is a nice boy, Gerald, and very talented with a wonderful future ahead in the art world. It would be nice if we invited him to call on Arienne when we settled back in Philadelphia."

"What did you say his name was again?"

"Matthew Gallio."

"Gallio, huh. Sounds like an Italian name to me."

"Well, yes...it is Italian, but does that make any difference?"

"It might make a lot of difference. I hadn't pictured Arienne being attached to an immigrant boy."

"Why Gerald! I had no idea you were so prejudiced."

"I think we had better discuss this further when we get back home." Gerald closed the subject, as he was so good at doing.

****

Matthew was already busy at work in Arthur Cowan's studio. He found it difficult to concentrate because he could not see Arienne. To help his frustration, he started a large portrait of Arienne as he remembered her from the first time he saw her standing above him at the mountain stream. In the painting, he had her sitting on a log with her feet bare, a lovely white dress spread around her on the ground, one hand dipping into the clear water. The sun was shining on her golden hair, while a sweet smile played upon her pink lips. It was halfway finished before Matthew received any word from her or Clarinda.

Arthur brought him the first unhappy news from the Bartholomews. Clarinda had suffered a severe stroke. Poor Arthur was hardly able to speak about it without tears. He hurried to the Philadelphia home only to be told that she was not seeing visitors. Matthew knew it would be impossible for him to gain entrance to the house if Arthur was refused admittance.

His heart was breaking for Arienne. How was he to see her under the circumstances? His wait was not for long.

Approximately a month after Clarinda was stricken, he picked up the Philadelphia newspaper to find a brief notice in the social column: *Mr. Gerald Bartholomew and his daughter Arienne have departed on a tour of Europe aboard the U.S.S. Phoenix. They expect to be abroad for the next seven months.*

Gallio could not believe his eyes. It couldn't be! Within days a note was delivered to him by Arthur.

"I swore I would never tell anyone about this note to you. Arienne slipped it to me the last time I stopped to see her grandmother."

The small vellum envelope carried her only note to Matthew:

> *My Darling:*
> *Father is insisting on taking me away. He knows I love you but says I will get over it. I never will, my dear. Without grandmother to help me, I cannot struggle against father. Perhaps the day will come when we can be together. I don't know. I only know that I will always love you, no matter what.*
>
> *Yours,*
> *Arienne*

Matthew felt sure his life would never be the same. He struggled to finish the portrait, which was destined to change his life even more.

Clarinda Bartholomew's death brought to an end the dreams of a young boy and was replaced with the determination of a strong young man. There were more surprises Matthew would have never thought possible for him. The mystery of why Clarinda willed the rambling lodge in the mountains to him he could not answer, but he took it with gratitude and grace.

She also left him a large trust to help keep the lodge, the bulk of which he would not realize until he was thirty years old. At first he wanted to refuse it all because of Arienne, but when she and her father didn't return for Clarinda's funeral, Arthur persuaded him that it was her fond wish that he keep the legacy to further his career.

****

Spring was once again blooming on the mountain. The winter snows had melted, washing the face of the hills with verdancy such as Gallio had never remembered. It was to be the beginning of his life at the lodge, but he fretted to himself about how he would ever keep the big house going. He asked Julia Keep if she would consider coming to work for him, but the financial sacrifice would have been too much to survive and still help her family. Gallio decided to contact his sister Teresa to inquire if she was, by chance, free to come and keep house for him.

Teresa arrived while the dogwoods were still in bloom. Brother and sister cried in each other's arms. She had left the cruel Jim Bird long ago.

Chapter 14: Searching

IF MATTHEW SEEMED to move with aplomb through the tragedies that plagued him during the last two years, it was not so.

Teresa watched him eat less and less as the weeks wore on at Queen's Escape. She tried encouraging him by cooking all of the foods *he* had always liked, to no avail.

At night the big house on the mountain took on an eerie look as lamplight reflected from room to room most of the night. He walked the floor. It was as if he was constantly trying to work out something in his mind.

Seeing no friends, losing weight at an alarming rate, and painting on the portrait of Arienne in a frenzied manner...he repainted over and over for whatever perfection he aimed for.

Finally Teresa wrote to Arthur Cowan about her brother's behavior, asking him to come.

Arthur was awed by the beauty of the lodge that was set on a shelf of the mountain, but he feared for the sanity of his young protégé when he saw him.

Matthew was at work in his studio when Arthur arrived.

Frenzied, could be the only word to describe the young man's activity. Teresa ushered Arthur into the studio.

"Matthew, someone's here to see you."

"Don't want to see anyone—I've told you...." He turned to see Cowan smiling at him, his hand outstretched.

"Oh, Arthur, I'm so pleased to see you here." His knees visibly weakened a little. "What brings you up here this time of the year?"

"I decided I needed a vacation away from the students. One of my advanced students agreed to take over for me for a while."

"Sit, sit down while I clean my brushes, then I'll show you around the place." Gallio busily cleaned his tools.

"Before we do that, I must look at your newest project here, Matthew; this portrait of Arienne is magnificent." He stood up and gazed closely at the painting."It will, of course, be the focal point of your next showing...or didn't I tell you, Daly Galleries wants to have another show of your paintings."

"No! I don't intend to have another show!"

"Come on, Matthew, show me the rest of the lodge, and the grounds. Let's talk about business later." Arthur patted his friend on the shoulder as they left the studio.

The tour of the house was long and quiet, but when they left the house, strolling the grounds, approaching the stream where Arienne and Matthew had met, Gallio became flushed. He was almost inarticulate. Observing Gallio, Arthur felt that his friend was either in need of a change or a doctor, or both.

****

Within the next few days, Arthur persuaded Matthew to leave the lodge for a brief visit to Cowan House and a visit to Arienne's home in Philadelphia. The idea of being around the home where his love had been raised was the deciding factor that led to his departure from Franklinton with Arthur.

They had hardly settled into their rooms again when Gallio arranged for Mose to drive him into the city to the Bartholomew house. Matthew walked up the few steps to the sturdy mahogany front door, where he lifted the heavy, brass door knocker and knocked impatiently. The butler answered the door with a questioning look on his face. "Yes sir?"

"My name is Matthew Gallio, and I have stopped in to inquire about the well-being of Mr. Bartholomew and his daughter Arienne."

"Oh yes, please come in and be seated," he indicated a chair not far from the door. "Please wait a moment." He disappeared into the rear of the house, giving Matthew a few minutes to observe the interior of the lavish townhouse entry hall with its massive mahogany and walnut furnishings, some of which were polished to a mirror sheen.

Beautiful tapestries and boldly framed painted faces of past Bartholomews hung upon the stairway walls. In the center of the entry room, and it was really too large to be called an entry hall, stood a marvelous round rosewood table polished so highly that the golden chrysanthemums in the crystal vase in its center were duplicated in the reflection on the table. The house was breathtaking, but it had already become quietly empty and vacant smelling.

Matthew had not been seated long when another servant, a woman of middle age, came from the rear of the house. "Please, Mr. Gallio, if you will follow me." Matthew left his coat and hat where it lay on the arm of the chair and followed her up the wide staircase.

She led him into a small sitting room, which Gallio immediately sensed, had been Clarinda Bartholomew's. The paintings on the walls all bespoke of her taste, and the dainty furniture coverings, too, told him who the room belonged to. The woman asked him to make himself comfortable for a moment while she went to a small desk with many drawers that was set in front of the windows overlooking the gardens. She pulled out a lower drawer and lifted a white envelope from its depths. "Mrs. Bartholomew said you were to get this."

"But...how could she know I would be here?"

"She said you would come someday soon." The servant left Matthew alone.

In the envelope was a brief note written with a shaking hand:

> *My dear protégé, yes my protégé, for it is I who have sponsored you all these years.*
>
> *I know how much you love my darling Arienne. She has told me much about you. I do not know where Gerald has hidden her in*

Europe, but I received the enclosed contents of this envelope shortly after their arrival in France. I'm sorry I could not help you more.

The note was simply initialed C.

Inside the envelope Matthew found a ragged piece of paper, obviously torn from a book's margin. It said simply: *Dearest Grandmother: He holds me captive with the nuns,* and scrunched down in the corner of the envelope was a tiny piece of pink satin baby ribbon. Gallio had no way of telling if the ribbon had been put there by Arienne or was there by happenstance.

He was devastated, unable to rise to leave the house for two hours. Mose led a half-dead man back to the carriage and drove him back to Cowan House.

****

The second showing of Matthew Gallio's work was held the following spring. Although it was attended by many more people than the first and was financially more successful, the magic had left the spirit of Gallio and he only went through the motions. The one thing that did gratify him was the extravagant praises that were reaped upon his portrait of Arienne. Offers to buy the painting ran high, but Matthew refused to part with it, instead, planning to hang it above the huge fireplace in the great-room of the lodge in Franklinton. It was titled *The Pink Ribbon*, and the one great curiosity that baffled observers was the lovely piece of pink satin ribbon that was held in her dainty hand. He never told anyone what the ribbon signified.

He wasn't sure himself.

****

As spring grew into summer, Matthew spent more and more time at the lodge painting. He found more peace there than at any other place. Arthur visited as often as possible and felt easier about Matthew's getting back to work. Gallio started to venture into the village more, and more, finding solace in old places and old school friends. He painted many of the children of the town but avoided portraits of the well-to-do.

Matthew started disappearing from the lodge for days at a time, but Teresa never questioned him about his comings and goings. She felt he was now a grown man and should know his own mind. But her curiosity was boundless as to where he went. She noticed, too, that when he returned, his clothes were unkempt and his face pallid. He soon returned to his usual habits so she kept quiet about it.

Established in the state as a fine portrait artist, there were many bids made upon his time. It was fast becoming a fad for the rich to brag that they were being painted by Gallio. Arthur knew it was only a matter of time before Matthew became nationally known and would be asked to paint the portraits of the famous.

His odd habits continued. He went away more and more, causing Teresa much worry. If it was not for the trust that was set up by Clarinda for the upkeep of Queen's Escape, they might have had a problem paying for everything since Matthew's income was becoming more and more limited due to his absences.

There was no one Teresa felt she could go to except, perhaps, Agatha Glenn. She thought about that and decided to go to Glenn House and see if Agatha could counsel her. Millie answered the door, inviting Teresa into the house.

"Why, Missus Bird, it's been a long time since you've been here...welcome." Her face went scarlet when she realized how she'd spoken so familiarly to Teresa. "Beg your pardon, ma'am, I'm just so surprised to see you again!"

"Don't be silly. Weren't we work partners here at one time? Is Missus Glenn in?"

"Yes, ma'am, just a moment."

Agatha, wearing her usual understated brownish dress, bustled into the hallway. "Teresa! It's so good to see you again. Come in and we'll have tea and chat."

It was Teresa's turn to blush. Being treated as an equal at the Glenn's was a new feeling. "I don't want to put you out, Ma'am."

"Nonsense! You're not putting me out, I'm quite alone today and feeling lonely." After they were seated in the parlor, Agatha seemed eager to chat. "Dolly's visiting a girlfriend for the day. They're probably planning the dresses they will wear for their graduation ceremony. She finishes school this year and is talking about entering a business school in Philadelphia to become a secretary. Have you ever heard of anything so absurd?"

"Girls are becoming more independent with each year, I guess." Teresa did not want to take sides.

"Perhaps you're right. Now tell me how things are going for you at the lodge. I understand that you are Gallio's main housekeeper. I think it is wonderful that you have come back here, especially since he needs you now so much."

"Things are going good, but I must admit I need some advice. That's why I've come here today, Missus Glenn. You have always been very kind to my family..."

"Dear child, I'm always here to help. What on earth could make you look so sad. Is that awful Jim Bird making trouble for you again?"

"No Ma'am! Jim Bird is out of my life forever."

"Good riddance to bad rubbish, I say. Now what can I help you with?"

Pools of tears started to run from under Teresa's eyelids unbidden. She tried to wipe them away quickly, but it was no use; they kept coming.

Agatha quickly handed her a lace hankie from her pocket. "Here, dear child, it can't be that bad."

"Oh, but it is! Matthew has started disappearing from the lodge for days at a time, and I don't know where he is or what to do."

Agatha sipped at her tea. "He always comes back?"

"Yes, so far he returns after a few days, but he looks awful when he does."

"You know I think of you as a member of our family, Teresa, but I can't think of a thing that I can do to solve this mystery for you...unless..." She stopped talking and set her tea cup down. "There is one possibility. I really hesitate to suggest..."

"Oh, please, missus Glenn; anything you can say to help will be appreciated."

"Well...have you thought about the possibility of having him followed when he leaves? I hate being devious."

Teresa's eyes grew large. "I never really considered it; besides I wouldn't know who to ask to do that."

"Now, now, Teresa, don't worry further. The next time you sense that Matthew is leaving, come down here to me and I'll take care of that." Agatha did love being considered helpful.

The young woman left Glenn House feeling much better, and the idea that she had some moral support made her days brighter.

****

It was exactly two weeks later that Matthew packed his small overnight kit for traveling again. Teresa spied from the hallway as he prepared to leave. He would have to ride his horse down the mountain trail toward town before he could prod his horse up the other side of the mountain to leave

Franklinton. He never left at night so she was sure that she had until the next morning to alert Agatha.

After dinner, she left the lodge and ran like a deer through the fallen leaves of autumn, down the familiar mountain path to Glenn House. Exhausted and dusty, she knocked at the door, hoping Agatha would answer her knock. She did.

"He's leaving in the morning..." she babbled breathlessly.

"All right, child, now settle down. I'll take care of it. Go home and try to relax; it won't do for us to be seen together tonight." Teresa nodded and wearily made her way back up the path.

The morning brought a steady rain that promised to stay all day. Matthew put on his slicker and mounted his horse without saying anything to his sister. He was out of sight, down the trail in no time.

Chapter 15: Directions

IT WAS SEVERAL DAYS before Teresa received any word from Agatha concerning their mutual plan to have Matthew followed. In the meantime, she was busy going through his desk trying to find a clue that would reveal the cause of her brother's behavior.

She read the note from Clarinda, which the woman had written to him before she died. Teresa wept for her brother's sorrow. Attached to the note was another paper clipping from the Philadelphia newspaper, which she had not seen.

It read:

Paris. Financier Gerald Bartholomew of Philadelphia was found dead in his hotel room, the victim of a heart attack. His attorney J.Q. Portman is handling arrangements.

Not a word about Arienne. So the mystery remained unsolved.

Teresa's heart ached for her brother. No wonder he was wracked by depression. He'd run up against a blank wall.

It had been a week since Gallio left the lodge when Agatha sent word for Teresa to come to the Glenn house.

The two women seated themselves in the parlor. "This will not please you, Teresa. Matthew is carousing and gambling his good money away in Pithole, that terrible oil town, up in the hills. I am told he seems all but lost of his senses at times. When he passes out from drink, the proprietor of the gambling house puts him in a room to sleep it off, and then he starts it all over again until he's broke and has to return home.

Teresa sat rocking and moaning softly like a wounded dog. "Oh, how I wish Father Cassidy was here. He'd know what to do." Agatha just shook her head, unable to help.

****

Goldy's graduation from Miss Simon's was quiet and speedy. She issued no invitations, neither did she tarry after she received her diploma.

James Peabody, expecting to hear from her after she graduated, heard nothing. When he returned to Pittsburgh after the spring semester at Princeton, his inquiries about Goldy went unanswered. No one seemed to have any idea about where she was. James' letters to Matthew requesting any news of her lay unopened on Gallio's desk, as did most of the artist's correspondence.

Goldy Wojna seemed to have disappeared. Her parents were packed and moved out of Franklinton by the middle of June. No one there had heard where they were going. There was speculation, among the townspeople, that they might have gone back to Poland.

The truth was that Goldy had started a new life with her parents—a life in which she was determined to find success.

The town was small but busy, noisy and growing, just the kind of place Goldy wanted to invest her well saved money. She'd squirreled away almost every cent she could from her monthly stipend that was sent to her from the Glenns, sometimes denying herself even necessities to get a few extra dollars into her bank account. Making do, mending, and in general, pinching every penny. It had all paid off. She was able to move to Oilton, Pennsylvania, where she put down a healthy down payment on the local hotel that was languishing from lack of management.

Moving her mother and father into the hotel as housekeeper and manager solved the problem of paying help that was undependable. The three of them had one common goal, and that was to make the Royal Hotel a moneymaker.

The oil industry was being born in the hills of northern Pennsylvania. Every day, news of a new well coming in was discussed over every bar and dining table. Barges were floating down the Allegheny River loaded with barrels of the crude oil headed for busy cities greedy for the new commodity. Fortunes were made overnight and sometimes lost just as fast. People were sinking wells in every piece of land they had available. Oilton was a way station on the route to Pittsburgh.

It didn't take Goldy long to figure out that the real money was going to be in oil. Six months after moving into the Royal Hotel and making sure her parents had the place well under control and paying, she quietly bought a silent partnership in a new gambling casino in Pithole—her name to be used only on the legal documents of ownership. The newfound-rich oil men who stopped briefly in their quest for more wells, or felt they were "fixed" for life, were ripe for the pickins at the Pithole Casino. Many a new deed was thrown on the table at the roulette wheel, the crap table, or the poker games. It was a rowdy, muddy town filled with the riff-raff of the countryside mixed with the slickers from the big cities. No one suspected that a "lady" was, in fact, controlling much of the wealth that rolled into Pithole on the stream of crude oil.

Goldy's partner Jeb Crane, a local man, was so happy with the wealth he was accruing that he didn't even begrudge turning over half of the take, each week, to a young messenger from Oilton. He had never met his silent partner, Goldy Wojna.

Meanwhile the sedate hotel owner went about her business of running a ladies millinery shop in the center of Oilton, where she barely broke even.

Sundays found the Wojna family walking to mass. Goldy was thankful for the many blessings she and her family had. The Wojnas had enough money and prestige to warrant their own pew, in the front of the sanctuary.

Leaving mass one Sunday, Goldy was brought up short to find James Peabody standing in front of the church. He was dressed impeccably as always, removing his hat as he approached her.

"My goodness!" She fluttered as her cheeks became pink. "What on earth are you doing here?"

"I might ask you that very question."

"This is where I live now, James, and...and may I introduce you to my mother and father, Rachel and Edward Wojna." Her parents shook hands amiably with James then seeming to sense that they were not needed at the meeting, excused themselves, walking toward the hotel.

"Why, Goldy?"

"Why what?"

"Why did you run away without a word?"

"I didn't run away...there were things I had to do. Business, to take care of, and of course, my parents to care for."

"It seems that you've accomplished just about all you've set out to do from what I've heard around town here. After inquiring after you, I was told you own half the town!"

"That's silly. I own the hotel and a millinery shop, which is barely making it. That's certainly not half the town."

She managed to laugh a little.

"May I walk you home?"

"Yes, of course, and you must stay for dinner. Mother is a wonderful cook." They strolled arm in arm toward the hotel.

"We live on the top floor," she explained to his questioning eyes. "It's quite spacious for the three of us."

As they climbed to the fourth floor, James wondered at the change in this girl since he last saw her. This was a woman of independence, not the nervous, unsure school girl he had fallen in love with.

The suite the Wojnas lived in was tastefully furnished, almost richly furnished, and held no hint of the mining-town hovel they had once occupied.

James was given one of the better suites in the hotel for his visit. Goldy didn't know quite how to handle the problem of telling him that there was no hope for their relationship.

She had already made up her mind never to marry, but she was afraid she could never make James understand why without revealing her whole miserable past, including the loss of the baby and her love for Matthew Gallio. She didn't want to hurt him either, but to extricate herself without hurting him seemed impossible.

****

Summer was lengthening into a rainy early fall. James had been in Oilton for a week, during which he and Goldy had started to take carriage rides around the countryside when the weather permitted. During one such ride, James stopped the horse under a sheltering maple tree and faced the woman he loved, determined to settle the issues between them.

"You know that I love you." He took her hand in his, bringing it up to his lips. "You must also know that I want you to marry me. You are very dear to me, but I am not a fool, my dear. I am not sure that you have any of these feelings for me." Goldy would not look into his eyes; instead she kept her face turned away.

James reached over across her and turned her body around, making it impossible for her to avoid his scrutiny. "Even if you do not love me now, I believe that love can grow between us, if you'll marry me. I have enough love for you for the two of us."

"I don't know what to say, James. I am very fond of you and feel great respect for you. I'm honored that you would even consider having me as your wife, but is that enough? I don't know that it is." Finally she raised her lovely blue eyes and looked into his that revealed the pain he felt. "Can't we just be friends? I mean at least for a while. There are many things that I must settle in my mind before I ever consider marrying."

"Is it hopeless then?" James pulled her toward him, holding her against his heart.

"No...No, I don't mean it is hopeless, my dear friend, but there are many things you do not know about me. I must have time to think about all this. After all, we are still very young and have plenty of time to plan."

James left town the next day feeling that things could not be too much worse, but still holding hope in his heart for a reconciliation and a marriage.

For weeks after James Peabody left town, Goldy kept to herself, talking little to anyone. Perhaps, she thought, she should not have been so quick to put James Peabody off. After all, love wasn't everything— or was it?

It was only by chance that Matthew Gallio's name once more entered Goldy's life. The messenger responsible for carrying her money from Pithole to her hands each week happened to mention that he had heard that a famous artist was hanging out at the casino in Pithole. He had also heard that he was drunk most of the time and that Jeb Crane was keeping a room for him in the casino so he could bleed him of all of his money.

Goldy felt her head start to swirl and she clung to the edge of a counter so she wouldn't fall down.

"Are you all right, ma'am?" The messenger boy reached out to support her.

Gathering her wits about her, she straightened up saying, "Yes, I'll be fine, you go on." She closed the shop and hurried as fast as she could toward the hotel. Finding her mother behind the front desk, she explained to her that a trip to Pithole was very necessary for business reasons. Goldy wanted to keep her knowledge about Matthew to herself.

Dressing herself in her finest traveling suit, Goldy packed a small bag and walked quickly to the stagecoach station to catch the afternoon coach to Pithole. It would take her a couple of weary, bumpy hours in the horse-drawn stagecoach to complete her trip to Pithole.

The town could be heard before it could be seen. Gunshots, yelling, and just general raucous noise announced the muddy cradle of the oil digs. Streets never meant for human feet were six inches deep in mud. If you were careful, you could pick your way along the main part of town on dozens of flat boards laid across rutted, mucky roads.

The coach carrying Goldy pulled up in front of the one hotel.

"Can you unload my bag for me?' she called up to the driver. The answer came as a thud at her feet; it had barely missed her head. Picking up the bag, she tried to get her bearings, deciding to head for the rear door of the Pithole Casino. It was certainly closer than the main entrance and required crossing only one narrow lane.

Leaving her bag at the hotel, she wobbled across a large plank that served as a walkway over the muddy thoroughfare, but she made a misstep and fell full length into the muck. Four unkempt men sitting on a nearby bench jumped up and down hooting and hollering, pointing fingers at her predicament. "What's wrong with you idiots? Can't you help a lady?"

"Oh, it's a lady is it? Kinda hard to tell," one of the loafers yelled. Another mooed like a cow, "Thought it was a muddy heifer lost its path." There was more hooting and yelling as Goldy pulled herself across to the other side of the street.

"You, dolts! You'd better hope that I never find out who you are." She shook globs of mud off her hands, pulling her skirt along behind her.

Reaching the back door to the casino, she tried the door. Locked. Then she began pounding with both fists and kicking the door. Finally someone opened it.

Jeb Crane stood holding the door knob, both eyes bulging, his mouth open. "Whaaaaa..."

"Don't start asking stupid questions, Mr. Crane, just help me in." Goldy stepped over the threshold.

"But, but..." Jeb didn't move.

"Now look here, Mr. Crane, I'm Goldy Wojna, your silent partner in these digs, and I'm not of a mind...in my condition, to listen to your grunts and questions. CLOSE THE DOOR!"

Jeb did just as he was told, a look of total surprise on his gaunt face. The skinny little man was dressed like a man of means...diamond stick pin and all. "Miz Wojna, forgive me, but what on earth happened to you?"

"It's pretty plain to see...I fell into the muddy street while four hyenas stood laughing at me!" Goldy started scraping goo from the front of her dress.

'I'm sorry about your accident, Miz Goldy... er...Miz Wojna. Just stand there a minute. I'll get Crystal to help you."

"Crystal? Who's Crystal?"

"She's one of my dealers...our dealer." He stuck his head through the open doorway calling for Crystal. The casino was empty, the gambling tables quiet until evening. Only a few drinkers leaned against the long wooden bar.

A frowsy looking woman, about forty, with blonde frizzy hair and painted cheeks came running, her red kimono partially open, showing her corset.

"Crystal, take Miz Wojna upstairs to a room where she can wash up and give her a nice dress to wear while her things are being cleaned up."

"Yes sir, I'll take care of it."

As the two women left the office, Goldy turned toward Jeb. "Don't you get lost. I want to talk to you about a serious matter."

"Yes Ma'am, I'll be around." He closed the office door with a heavy sigh.

Half an hour later, Goldy stood in front of a murky wall mirror in Crystal's room looking at herself. The dress she had on was a bruising purple skin-tight number covered with flashing bugle beads of the same color dripping from what could loosely be referred to as the bodice. Her breasts were only partially covered, dangerously close to falling out of the top. It was so tight around the hips it promised little or nothing underneath. "Haven't you got something a bit plainer?" she asked the dealer.

"No ma'am. I've given you the best dress I own!"

Feeling ungrateful for Crystal's generosity, she told the woman it would be fine until her things were cleaned. Wobbling around in the bar girl's high-heeled shoes was a struggle. Goldy headed for the stairs that led down to the casino.

Clutching the wooden banister as tightly as possible, she took one step at a time, very slowly. The few men at the bar followed her progress with mixed facial reactions...surprise, lust, fascination, and amusement.

When she was halfway down the stairs, she spotted James Peabody, hat in hand, watching her entrance on the scene.

Leaning over the railing, holding up her breasts, she called out to him, "What are you doing here, James Peabody?"

"Looking for you. I thought..."

"Well, if you're feeling helpful, why not come up here and help me down the stairs before I break my neck?"

James dropped his hat on a nearby table and scrambled up the steps. He picked Goldy up and carried her down to the bottom of the steps, where he stood holding her.

"Put me down!"

"Must I?"

"Now really, James, this has been enough of a show."

Motioning with her head, she demanded he set her on her feet. The watchers at the bar still looked on with interest. Hurriedly, she pulled James into Jeb Crane's office, slamming the door after them.

Jeb was nowhere in sight as Goldy approached his big desk.

"I told that man to stay here until I came back," she muttered to herself.

James continued to stare at her. "You know you don't have to bring yourself down to this kind of work to get by."

"What are you talking about?"

"This place, that dress...working as a bar girl. My God! Goldy, you're an educated girl. I won't allow you to do this!"

Goldy's face went absolutely pale. "You're a fool James Peabody! A damned fool! I'll have you know that I don't work here and this dress is borrowed because I fell into the mud in my clothes."

"Oh!" James sat down in the nearest chair. "But why should you even be in such a place as this?"

"What, may I ask, are you doing here?" She stood over him, both hands on her hips.

"I went to Oilton to see you; your mother told me you'd gone to Pithole on business. Funny business if you ask me for a girl like you."

"Following me around, I don't appreciate that at all. Why should I have to explain my actions to you? You don't own me!"

"You're right, but I do love you."

That quieted her down a bit. Still, she resented him putting his nose in her business.

"Let me take care of you, Goldy."

"I don't need anyone to take care of me. I want you to know I came here on real business because I happen to own half of this casino and, furthermore, I own several more properties here in Pithole. I'm rich....James Peabody....I'm a rich woman and no thanks to anyone but myself. I don't need a keeper!"

Then she started to cry. With every sob, the bugle beads shimmered more.

James jumped up to take her in his arms. A smile on his face broadened with the twinkle in his eyes. "Is your business completed here?"

"Not quite."

"Then let's get it over with and go back to Oilton. I still have a day to spend with you." Offering his handkerchief to her, she dabbed at her nose. Holding her tenderly, his lips found hers in a long gentle kiss.

In private, Jeb Crane got his orders from his not so silent partner about how to treat Matthew Gallio. No more milking the artist dry, and whatever Gallio lost was to be back in his saddle bag before he left to return home.

Chapter 16: Broken Dreams

AGATHA SELDOM spent time in her tower room anymore. Conrad seemed to be busy at the mines most of the time. They spoke very little except over the dinner table, and even then he seemed distracted, talking to her about politics and the need for the government to stockpile coal reserves against a possible civil uprising. Agatha understood nothing about those things.

To her surprise, one evening he asked her if she had heard from Jordan recently. He was still in the west at Walter Glenn's spread—Walter, of course, being Conrad's brother.

"Has Jordan contacted you lately, Agatha?"

She hesitated at first, hoping to avoid any argument. "Yes. He wrote about two weeks ago."

"And?"

"Well, things aren't much to his liking out there."

"Why doesn't that surprise me? Has my brother written to us about him at all?"

"No. Walter hasn't contacted us about Jordan. I had hoped that the western life would help settle Jordan a bit."

"At least it's good news that Walter is, apparently, still tolerating him. I'd have thought he would have kicked him out by now."

Agatha bit her tongue, sensing an unpleasant confrontation about Jordan. It always seemed to go that way when they discussed their son. No matter what, she still missed him terribly.

Dolly sat at the table during this exchange, quietly hoping the conversation would end before it got around to her.

Conrad looked at his daughter with a stern eye. "Are you still planning on going to Philadelphia to that damned secretarial school, or have you come to your senses?"

"Now, Conrad, don't be so hard on Dolly. She's just trying to plan a future for herself. After all, it is what a lot of the girls try to do nowadays."

"Poppycock! She doesn't need to be tromping off. I can give her work to do if that's what she wants. Anyway, she should be thinking about getting married and settling down."

With that, Dolly slammed her fork onto her plate. "And just where am I supposed to find a husband around here? Among the miners, maybe?" She flounced out of the dining room, and her footsteps could be heard racing up the stairs, to her room.

"Conrad, why not leave Dolly alone? She has a right to get educated if that's what she wants." There was silence during the rest of the meal.

After dinner, while Millie cleared the table, Agatha quietly climbed the stairs to Dolly's room. The girl was lying across her bed, face down, sobbing.

"Don't cry, darling; your dad is just upset and overworked. I'm sure he didn't really mean to hurt you." Agatha leaned over her daughter, smoothing her lovely auburn hair.

Dolly continued to sob, her shoulders shaking. "He just doesn't understand. No one understands. I have to get away from here before I lose my mind."

"Oh please, dear, don't talk like that. Things can't be that bad; after all, you are well cared for here."

"Mother, it's just like it always was. You never would listen to me...never let me tell you what was wrong, never. Always Jordan was all that mattered. Jordan could do no wrong."

"That's not true!" Agatha felt stunned by the accusation. "I love you...I always have."

"If you only knew me, Mother, you might understand why I can't stay here. There's no future for me here. Who would ever want me for a bride?" Her face was only a few inches from Agatha's as she raised herself up from the bed and ran from the room.

Her mother, stunned by the accusations and confused by the conversation, sat on the edge of her daughter's bed, her face in her hands, wondering how she could have failed the child. What did Dolly mean that no one would want her?

****

The train ride down the mountain to Philadelphia meant freedom for Dolly Glenn. As the wheels of the train clacked out their steel rhythm, she kept repeating over and over to herself, a new life...a new life...a new life...a new chance.

Dolly's departure from the Glenn's house not only left Agatha bereft and lonely, it had caused a subtle change in her relationship with Conrad. The distance between them became wider and quieter. Agatha took on more philanthropic projects and spent more time with her church groups. Conrad only immersed himself deeper in his work. The big white house, which had been such a hub of activity and was so full of living, stood like a quiet observer in the town.

Chapter 17: Nightmares

THE MOUNTAINS were beautiful in the snow, making Queen's Escape look like a Christmas card picture. Matthew stopped his frequent visits to Pithole, remaining busy in his studio, with infrequent visits to Arthur Cowan's estate.

The civil uprising foretold by Conrad Glenn seemed more imminent with each passing day. Feelings against slavery were being discussed often and more loudly with each speech in the United States Senate. President Lincoln had already made it clear how much he despised slavery in the south. The south, dominated by owners of large plantations, felt that their very way of life was being threatened. Secession from the Union was considered more seriously with each political move toward abolition. The call to arms from both the North and the South was being heard by all.

Gallio, at twenty-one, paid little attention to politics, but James Peabody, urged on by his father's hawkish attitude toward taking up arms, which had more to do with fuel profits than patriotism, volunteered for the army. He was given a commission as a captain in the 149th Regiment—The Pennsylvania Bucktail Regiment, so named for the white piece of furry deer skin they attached to their hats.

September 23rd, 1862, was his last furlough before being actively called to duty. He rode the train to Oilton. Goldy waited at the station, hardly aware of the dangers he would be facing before they would meet again...if they ever did.

She waved her lace handkerchief at him when he stepped down from the railroad car.

"Over here, James," she called. He pushed through the crowd of departing soldiers that were on the platform.

"Goldy, it's so good to hold you again." He hugged her small frame against him. It's been too long, and now this... having to separate again." His lips were warm against hers as she returned his kiss.

"You look wonderful, James. Your uniform suits you...so handsome." The two started to walk toward the hotel, arm in arm. "We've put you in the bridal suite." She laughed.

As they walked, time seemed to stand still for James. "Have you reconsidered my proposal at all?" He squeezed her tiny waist closer.

"Let's not spoil the two days we have with all of that serious talk." Goldy looked up into his eager face. "Let's just be happy for these two days so that we'll both have wonderful memories of our time together."

There were carriage rides into the countryside, picnics, and dancing as Mrs. Wojna played the piano in the hotel dining room. Goldy had planned her wardrobe for the visit carefully, wearing all of the colors that best suited her. As always, James was dazzled.

The last evening, before the train arrived to carry him into action, they stood strangely silent and Goldy wished that she truly loved him as she loved Matthew Gallio. But unknown to James, Matthew always stood between them.

As they stood on the station platform, they kissed. Goldy placed a small package in his hand. After the train had left Oilton, he opened it.

It was the magnificent miniature portrait of Goldy that Gallio had painted for her. James pressed it close to his heart before he pocketed the treasure.

Matthew joined the Union Army in October of 1862 and was assigned to sketch battlefield scenes for the government to release to newspapers. Although he saw much of the action, he was not participating himself. Many of his battle scenes were to be held in high esteem.

****

The last days of June 1863 were hot and sticky. The southern army was pushing on toward Gettysburg, Pennsylvania, to bivouac in the town of Holidaysburg.

At three o'clock a.m., no one was around on the streets of Franklinton. Agatha had gone to bed late and Conrad was away on business. Dolly had surprised her mother with a quick visit that was to be for a week. The two women had sat up until almost eleven o'clock that night discussing Dolly's new job in Philadelphia and the news in town. As she prepared for bed, Agatha hadn't felt so happy in months.

A sudden sound jolted Agatha awake. She looked at the clock...three o'clock. Then again a strange sound, almost like a child being choked, had her alert. A thud against a wall followed and she got out of bed, put on her robe. She reached for the shotgun Conrad kept over the bedroom mantel. Silently, she crept down the hall.

Another thud and a muffled scream made her sure that the noise was coming from Dolly's bedroom. Lamplight shown beneath the partly closed door.

Holding the shotgun in both hands, she pushed the door open gently with her bare foot. The sight she beheld was horrible to see. A gray-clad rebel soldier was on top of Dolly, pinning her down on the bed tearing at her nightclothes.

The next move Agatha made was not silent, the floorboard creaked under her foot. The bewhiskered southern soldier staggered up off of the bed, his boots on the floor, giving Agatha a clear shot at him.

"NO! Mother, NOOOOO!" Dolly screamed.

But it was too late. The shot hit the rebel in the face and he fell forward on the bed as Dolly continued to scream. Agatha dropped the shotgun where she stood, her mouth agape. Lying there, streaming blood...half his face gone...was someone she felt she knew. Then with a closer look, she too screamed. It was Jordan......dead. Agatha suddenly understood what Dolly had never been able to tell her.

Her mind a blank, Agatha walked stiffly from the bedroom, down the long staircase, and out of the house, not stopping until she had reached Fred Slager's house. Looking like a ghost herself, she pounded on the door then waited for Slager to open the door.

"My God! Agatha! What's wrong?"

"You had better get the Sheriff, Fred. I've just shot Jordan!" Her knees buckled beneath her as Fred caught her before she hit the floor. He half carried her as he eased her toward the closest chair in the entry hall.

"Maybe you just had a nightmare, Agatha."

"I killed Jordan. He's at the house in a rebel uniform."

"This is crazy!"

"Yes. This is crazy...but it is true. Please Fred, you must send word to Pittsburgh to fetch Conrad." After that, she said nothing more, just stared into space.

Dolly was hurriedly changing her clothes, putting the torn nightgown into the back of her dresser drawer, trying not to look at the body of her brother stretched across her bed.

Blood seemed to be on everything in the room. After dressing, she ran downstairs out of the house and started down the porch steps. Suddenly her legs gave way, and reaching for the railing, she held on as everything went black. Dolly was unconscious when

Fred Slager and Sheriff VanDyke came up to the porch.

Fred, kneeling beside Dolly rubbing her wrists, working over the girl, wondered what would come of this tragedy.

Millie had awakened by then and took over the care of Dolly, cooing soft words, putting a shawl around the girl's shoulders.

Up in Dolly's bedroom VanDyke went about his business. Fred murmured, "Not very pretty, is it?"

"No. Not pretty at all." The sheriff wiped his forehead with his handkerchief.

Fred stayed close to the door. "What, in the name of God, do you think, happened here?"

"What's Jordan Glenn doing in a rebel uniform, and what's he doing here now?" VanDyke seemed to be talking to himself.

"You're not likely to get much information from the women tonight. Conrad should be back here tomorrow; maybe then we'll be able to make some sense of all this." Slager remained with the sheriff until the undertaker arrived to take the body away. The two men went back to Fred's office for a stiff drink from Slager's special stock that he kept in his desk drawer. They needed it.

Conrad Glenn arrived the next day on the early afternoon train. He hurried toward his home, leaving his luggage with the station master until later. A sense of foreboding was creeping up his back.

When he entered the house, he heard voices coming from the parlor. Agatha, Dolly, Fred Slager, and Sheriff VanDyke were all seated around the room awaiting his arrival. Dolly jumped up as soon as she saw her father and ran to him, throwing her arms around his neck. He kissed her on the cheek, taking her arms from around his neck. "Agatha..." he whispered as he walked toward his wife. She sat there like a marble statue, looking at the floor.

Fred rose, "Conrad, we're glad your back. We need you here." He took Conrad's arm, leading him toward a chair.

"Can someone tell me what this is all about? The telegram said only that there was trouble at home.... Sheriff VanDyke, what brings you here to my house?"

The sheriff held his hat between his fingers, turning the brim slowly as he began relating the events of the previous night. When he was finished, Conrad looked like someone had beaten him.

"We do not understand why Jordan was wearing a rebel uniform, or why he was here at that time of night at all."

Trying to keep his voice even, Conrad said, "I believe I can answer some of your questions. My brother Walter, in Texas, has been trying to keep Jordan interested in helping him on his spread. It wasn't going well between them. Jordan was totally undisciplined, as always. I received a letter from Walter some time ago, informing me that Jordan had run off. He threatened to join the Confederate Army. Walter couldn't stop him." He looked at Agatha who was staring at him in disbelief. Conrad put his head down in his hands. His shoulders shook with quiet sobs.

"Why didn't you tell me all of this?" Agatha spat the words like bullets at Conrad.

"I was afraid it would worry you more than you were already worried. I thought he would just head for home, as usual."

"Oh, Daddy..." Dolly started weeping again.

"He obviously joined the rebels just long enough to get close to home and then he must have deserted. I would expect that of Jordan." Conrad turned his head, trying to conceal the tears that were streaming down his cheeks.

Quietly, Agatha rose from her chair. "How can you talk like that when he lies dead." She slowly climbed the staircase to her room.

Jordan Glenn's killing was ruled accidental. The town whispered long about the shooting, never sure what really happened that night.

Conrad insisted that Dolly return to Philadelphia to her new job.

Agatha withdrew to her room, stepping onto the upstairs porch only rarely. The only persons she would see, other than Millie, were Dolly on her infrequent visits, and Teresa Bird, who joined her for tea in her upstairs room about once a month. She refused to talk to Conrad at all. Her frequent visits to Jordan's grave were usually late in the afternoon when no one was around at the cemetery. Always dressed in black, if she passed anyone at the grave site, she held her head down, unseeing.

Chapter 18: Distances

WORD OF JORDAN GLENN'S death reached Goldy several days after it happened. The news was repeated to her by an oil driller who passed through Franklinton the day after the tragedy.

How did she feel?...She asked herself that question. It had been a long time since she consciously thought about that terrible year Jordan Glenn had abused her. The nightmares, too, became infrequent, allowing her to sleep peacefully many nights.

Oddly enough, her first thoughts were for Agatha, knowing the suffering she must be going through. She felt sorry for the misled mother who, perhaps, loved too much. Goldy felt strangely light as if a large weight had been lifted from her shoulders. She unconsciously rubbed the shoulder that was scarred by the hoof of Jordan's stallion long ago. It is over, she thought, finally over.

Mail from the battlefields to the civilian population moved at a slow pace. A letter from James arrived for Goldy showing a post date several weeks old.

> *Dear Goldy:*
> *Just a note to tell you that I have been discharged from the army because of*

medical problems. I have returned to Pittsburgh but do not think I will be here very long. Business in New York City calls me there.

Sincerely hope you are well and happy. Perhaps we shall meet again before too long.

With Affection,
James

Perhaps we shall meet again! Goldy didn't understand that from a usually persistent suitor. It left her mystified and upset. Had he met someone else? If he did, he should say so. She tore the letter into little pieces. Still, she pondered the puzzle.

Matthew went into Philadelphia during the late summer of 1865. As usual, he spent his time at Arthur Cowan's. The Daly Gallery was once more planning a showing of Matthew's work.

He had been quite prolific since his return home from the army, gaining many new and important clients who wished to be immortalized by Gallio. But he was tired.

His appearance seemed to belie his twenty-five years. He had already started to gray at the temples, and his black curly hair peppered with steel gray made him look much older, but even more handsome.

Julian Daly sent invitations for the Gallio show to all the elite of Philadelphia and many in Pittsburgh.

The crowd that showed up for the showing were outfitted in colorful finery, eager to dress up again after the drab dressing during the war. They mulled over the portraits and studies, talking about the depth of character the artist brought to his work. They also buzzed about the prices of the works...a bit high, perhaps. Several nudes were included in the collection, making the party even livelier with the guests guessing who had really posed for them. They were sold quickly.

After the show, Matthew approached Arthur. "You know my life has been on hold for a long time, Arthur. I've decided to try once more to trace Arienne. Then perhaps I can rest."

"What are your plans?"

"I'm leaving for France next week. I intend to contact Gerald Bartholomew's lawyer in Paris to try and discover where Gerald put Arienne."

True to his word, Matthew boarded a ship the next week, headed for France. He registered at the Grand Hotel in Paris and started his search for J.Q. Portman. It took him only two hours of walking, talking, asking questions before he finally found himself in the outer office of the lawyer.

The secretary asked him to be seated as she announced his presence. After a lengthy wait, Portman greeted him at his office door, inviting him in. "Ah, Mister Gallio—be seated." He pointed to a chair opposite his desk. "How can I help you?"

"I have traveled from Philadelphia to ask you for information about Arienne Bartholomew." He felt his heart beating faster. Could this be the end of the long search?

"Of course, you are the artist. Mr. Bartholomew spoke of you briefly."

"Where is she?"

"What is she to you, sir?"

"We were engaged." Matthew looked down and bit his lip.

"Ah...I see. Since her father is dead, I suppose it would not matter if I told you what little I know. Mr. Bartholomew talked about a convent on the outskirts of Paris named Saint Celeste's. I can tell you how to get there, but it might be useless. I don't know."

After receiving the directions to the convent, Matthew raised himself wearily from the chair, thanking the lawyer for his help. Afraid to hope, he walked out into the sparkling city again, never noticing the beauty of the City of Lights. For him, there was only one important reason for him to be in France.

The buggy he had rented creaked and groaned over the ruts of the country road north of the city. Passing numerous old castle ruins, his eyes searched for a small forest known to be the location of the little stone convent called Saint Celeste's. It was hot, and sweat had stained his fine linen and suit coat. His eyes ached from the glare of the sun.

Almost like a mirage, there it was, nestled into a grove of trees, barely visible from the road. The natural fieldstone walls looked forbidding, and no life stirred around the place. Even the leaves on the trees seemed to be unmoving.

Matthew jumped down from the buggy and tied the old horse to the nearest tree. He would try to find some water for the mare later.

A small iron gate with rusted hinges presented the only access to the convent. A bell hung on a chain near the door. He shook the chain vigorously alarming the surroundings to life. Birds fluttered from trees, complaining in different sounds. It seemed like an hour, when actually it was about seven minutes, before he heard someone pull on the door. It creaked open like a rusty jar lid that had been forgotten in a damp cellar.

Standing before him was a tiny, wizened old nun, her habit of black and white starched to chafing stiffness. He couldn't help wondering if the habit held her up.

"Oui?" she addressed him."

"I would like to talk to the Mother Superior."

"Non English," she answered, then motioned him in. Pointing to a bench, she had him sit. Then with great effort, she pushed the iron gate shut. Again, she motioned for him to wait where he was.

Several minutes later, a tall nun, in a habit like the first, approached him. She had large searching eyes and a firm step. "I speak some English," she announced, folding her hands in front of her.

"Please, sister, my name is Matthew Gallio from America, and I am trying to find a young girl by the name of Arienne Bartholomew. I have been told that she might have been brought here by her father several years ago.

"Bartholomew...Bartholomew...it is a name I have heard before. She is...how you say...disappeared... not here anymore."

"Then she was here at one time?"

"Come with me, please." She led Matthew around the convent to the back of the building where there was a small cemetery. Continuing to walk, she stopped in front of a tiny carved stone that read simply BARTHOLOMEW on it. Matthew's face looked stricken. "Is this where she is buried?"

"Non, her child is...put...here. Arienne have... baby girl...not live."

"Oh! God!" Stunned, Matthew started to walk blindly toward the convent. He muttered. "There was a baby...our baby."

He stopped suddenly, turning toward the sister. "Where is she now?"

The tall nun's eyes were veiled and she looked at the ground. "Arienne is no more. I am sorry."

With that, Matthew once more walked back to the stone marker and wept openly for a long time.

"Come." The nun pulled on his arm, taking him into the convent where they entered a dimly lit chapel. "Sit, please. It is good for you to be here for some time before you leave."

Matthew, hardly conscious of where he was, sat quietly in the candlelit chapel for at least an hour before he stirred to leave that place of sorrow. Faint purple streaks of sunlight filtered through the stained-glass windows, making him remember Father Cassidy. How he wished he could talk with him now.

Deep red drapes covered the entrance to a place behind the altar where the priest's fittings were kept. They swayed slightly and a small nun's face could be seen near their closings. The face appeared, unseen by anyone, carefully hidden in the folds and shadows. It was a face Matthew would have known well as Arienne's, but now she was Sister Philipe.

The nun's face, behind the drape, could not take her eyes from the young man's face—to her, that beautiful face she dreamed about so many nights. But she had sinned, and after sinning, she had been punished by losing her wonderful baby girl. That she firmly believed, and taking her vows to the sisterhood was the only penance she could ever give for such a sin. Still, in her secret heart, she could not forget the love that had sustained her through their early separation and the birthing of the child. She searched his face for every line, every hue, as if she were devouring him, for she knew that she would never see the dear face again. Her tears flowed down her face and she could not stop them. Her love, her life before now, her everything would never know that she still lived and yet died.

Matthew got up from the pew and walked out of the chapel, never to know that Sister Philipe had watched him, hungered for him the whole time he had been there. He could only think it was over.

Chapter 19: Chances

ARTHUR COWAN waited for Matthew's ship in New York City. As he stood on the pier, looking for Gallio to appear, he wondered what news the young man would bring back from France. Then as he peered up at the gangplank, Matthew was there, head down, shoulders drooping. Arthur felt the news was not good. Matthew spotted his mentor, raising his hand in greeting. The two friends shook hands firmly. "It's good to see you back," Arthur patted his friend on the back.

"It's good to be back." He retrieved his baggage from a porter. After going through the necessary business at the port, the two men climbed into a waiting carriage and headed for the home of Arthur's friend Jacob Steele.

"You must tell me what happened, Matthew. I have thought of little else since you left."

"There isn't much to tell. Arienne is dead. It is finally all over." He had difficulty speaking of it further. His voice failed him. Gallio never spoke of Arienne again.

"Let's try and enjoy Jacob's hospitality until we leave for Philadelphia in a few days." The Matthew Gallio Arthur observed was no longer the lost, agonized person who had confided in him a month ago. This man was quiet, but his eyes were once more filled with life, not death. If he mourned, it would not destroy him again. He had gained a strength for himself.

The dinner at Jacob Steele's that evening was glittering, with diamond stickpins on the men and diamond necklaces on their spouses. Matthew and Arthur were the only men there who were not in dinner attire, but no one seemed to notice or care. Conversation flowed easily among the fourteen guests. Some were openly impressed to have Arthur Cowan and Gallio, two such well known artists, among them. Eagerly, they asked Matthew about his recent trip to Europe and his opinion of Paris. He answered that it was a business trip and that he was not there long enough to form an opinion.

"Did you bump into John Jay while you were there?" Jacob asked. "I've heard he is trying to drum up interest in getting contributors into a fund to build a big art museum here in New York."

"I really didn't see anyone of note," Matthew answered, hoping to end that part of the conversation.

As the men retired to the library, the butler led a new guest in. It was James Peabody. Matthew jumped up, totally surprised. "My God, James, it's a real treat to see you!" He threw his arms around James' shoulders. The crutch under James' arm fell to the floor with a bang. Gallio quickly picked it up. "It's so good to see you, old friend." Stepping back, Matthew was shocked to discover that his old friend had only one leg. He could have wept for James, but

Peabody stood there beaming at him in utter delight at meeting Gallio again.

The right leg of James' trousers was neatly pinned up. Seeing his friend's dismay, he patted his left leg. "I've still got one good pillar. Been here in New York to have a local fellow fashion some contraption to help me with a peg leg of some kind." He laughed.

The two old friends sat talking late into the evening about their travels with the army during the war. Parting, they promised each other to keep in touch better than in the past.

****

At twenty-four years of age, Goldy was beginning to feel as if her wealth could not be the only thing in her life to offer her happiness. She thought more frequently of the puzzling letter from James. The more she thought about it, the more curious she was, until one afternoon she decided to take a trip into Pittsburgh.

She told herself it was for business at the bank. In the back of her mind, she knew she was lying to herself. The opportunity to see James again was the real priority.

Goldy's arrival in Pittsburgh brought back memories of the first time she had come to the city. She had been an uneducated, insecure, abused young girl who was just daring to begin to hope for a better life. The woman who registered at the prestigious hotel that afternoon stood tall and straight, her chin forward and head held high, dressed in the latest fashion. A truly beautiful lady.

Hiring a carriage the next day, she ordered the driver to take her by the Peabody mansion. As they approached the house, she said, "Slow down driver; I like to look at lovely houses." No one was around. Back at the hotel, she arranged with the carriage driver to pick her up before lunch the next day.

"Take me to the finest restaurant in town for lunch, then wait," she ordered. The Penn Inn was, indeed, a fine restaurant, with the best of linen and silver. Waiters, looking like penguins in their black and white uniforms, were friendly, attentive, and quick to explain the French words on the menu. "I'll have fillet of sole with lemon-butter sauce and fresh garden peas," she ordered.

"Would Madam like an English tea?"

"Why yes, that would be good." Settled at the table, Goldy allowed her eyes to scan the dining room for any sign of James. He was not to be seen. Disappointed, she picked over her lunch, leaving most of it.

"Is the food not good?" the waiter asked.

"Oh, very good. I just find I'm not hungry." Paying her check, she hurried out the door toward the waiting carriage. "Drive me by the Peabody house again. I like the architecture," she fibbed.

As the carriage approached the house again, the front door opened, and a familiar figure stepped out gingerly. With one crutch, a man descended the few steps to the sidewalk. Unable to avoid detection,

Goldy held her parasol in front of her face, hoping the man would not see her. As the horses passed by, one of them side-stepped, making a fuss for some unknown reason. The man peered from under the brim of his hat. It was James. He quickly put his head down and turned it in the opposite direction.

I'll never forgive him for ignoring me like that, Goldy fumed as the carriage approached her hotel. He was walking with a crutch...what could be wrong with him? Why should I care? He obviously isn't worried about me or how I've managed all these months. Still...he seemed to have a lot of trouble walking...well, it's not my worry anymore! She paid the driver and hurried to her room. Packing her luggage as fast as she could, she was determined to board the late afternoon train back to Oilton.

Pittsburgh that afternoon was gray with clouds. She waited in her room for train time when a soft knock sounded on her door. "Yes," she called.

"Message," the answer came.

Quickly she opened the heavy oak door. The bellboy stood there, a small package in his hand. "A man in the lobby sent this up to you; he didn't leave a name."

Quickly she opened the small parcel. Inside was the beautiful miniature Gallio had painted of her. She ran after the boy. "Where is he? Is he still down there?"

"I don't know, ma'am."

The long staircase to the lobby seemed never-ending. Goldy pulled up her skirts, to better travel down them. When she got to the lobby, there was no one in sight. Approaching the desk, she asked, "Did you notice where Mr. Peabody went...the man with the crutch?"

"Why, yes ma'am. I believe he walked toward the park across the street."

She ran out of the lobby and rushed across the street as fast as she could run. He was sitting on a bench watching the ducks on a small, pond.

"James Peabody! How dare you leave without talking to me." She stood before him her small hands flying up and down in frustration. "The least you could do is tell me what I have done to deserve this kind of treatment!"

"My dear, please forgive me. I just didn't think you'd want me around anymore."

"Want you around! What on earth do you mean? First you write to me as if I were a stranger, then you ignore me."

"Believe me, my dear, I do not consider you a stranger."

"Then...then why?"

James struggled to get up, reaching for his crutch that was propped against the bench. When he was erect, he pulled his right trouser leg up a few inches, showing her the wooden leg he wore. "What would you want with me now?" He asked quietly.

Goldy felt as if she'd been struck in the heart. Her beautiful green eyes widened and teared. Instead of pity, she screamed at him, "How can you ever think of me as so shallow, so pitiful? I've never been in love with your damn leg!" She walked up close to him, looking into his eyes, "It's you I care for." Her arms were around his neck, her soft mouth on his trembling lips. For the first time, she knew she truly loved the man forever. Yes, Matthew Gallio had stood between them for a long time, and she knew he would always own a piece of her heart, but now as James held her against his heart, she knew he was her life.

Chapter 20: Matthew

THE WEDDING of Goldy Wojna and James Peabody was a small affair held in the garden of the Peabody mansion. Only the families and a few close friends were in attendance. They wanted it that way. Matthew felt that it was almost unreal that two of his best friends should have found each other. He was happy for them, but his thoughts lingered, momentarily, on Arienne and his own loneliness.

Goldy kissed him gently before she and James left in the carriage to begin a short honeymoon in Europe. She noticed a sadness in Matthew's eyes that hadn't been there before, but her thoughts did not stay with him long. Her eyes sparkled as she snuggled close to her new husband.

Matthew's trip back to Queen's Escape was his first since he had returned from Paris. His last few months had been spent in Philadelphia, where he had leased a large townhouse.

The house he leased, pinched into the center of a row, was a brick building on a short, dead-end street near Daly's Gallery. Gallio had spent the last few weeks furnishing the third floor studio with all of his painting needs.

As the rented buggy rolled up the road toward the huge lodge, Gallio realized how very glad he was to be back at Queen's Escape. His thoughts were turning toward the town and the people he hadn't seen for so long, and especially, he was anxious to see his dear sister again.

Teresa, expecting him, stood on the front porch watching the buggy approach, excitement on her face.

Matthew waved to her as he approached, thinking how mature she looked and how really pretty she had become. Her small stature belied her strength and determination. Black curls were springing loose from the sides of her chignon, closer inspection showing some prematurely gray hair at her temples. And why not, Matthew thought, after all she'd been through in her young life. There had been few rewards for Teresa. *I must paint a portrait of her soon,* he thought.

The brother and sister embraced on the porch. "I'm so glad you're home, Matthew, there is so much to catch up on."

"I'm glad to be here." He thought to himself, *I really am glad to be home.* As he entered the parlor, the portrait of Arienne that hung over the mantel caught his eye immediately. For a brief moment, great sadness came over him. It passed quickly.

"The house looks very nice, Teresa. You've done a wonderful job here."

"I've had little else to keep me busy, what with you traveling the world. The church ladies try to keep me working and I spend a little time with Agatha..." She stuttered at the familiar way she'd addressed Mrs. Glenn... "Agatha Glenn, I mean. She is still suffering great sorrow and guilt over Jordan's death. I'm one of the few people she'll allow to visit with her. She asks about you often. Perhaps you will be able to make a call on her before long?"

"Yes, of course, I'll do that. Now tell me what that wonderful aroma is that I smell coming from the kitchen."

"Cook's having a hey-day cooking up all the things that you like."

"Ummm, I can hardly wait."

"I hope you won't mind, Matthew, but I have invited Fred Slager to dine with us this evening." Teresa seemed very nervous.

"Fred? Why I haven't seen Fred Slager for a long time. It'll be nice to see him again." Teresa breathed a sigh of relief to herself.

The bank president arrived at the lodge promptly at six p.m. Teresa met him at the door, taking his hat and coat, then led him into the parlor, smiling up at him sweetly. "He's here, Matthew," she twittered a bit. Gallio was standing near the fireplace, a glass of wine in his hand. "Welcome, welcome Mr. Slager. Sit down. How about a glass of wine, or would you prefer something else?"

"Well, my boy, if you don't mind, I'd prefer a good stiff whiskey to help digest."

"Of course," Matthew chuckled.

Teresa watched the two men for a moment then excused herself to look after things in the kitchen.

Matthew thought he had never seen his sweet sister looking so happy...a strange word for Teresa, but it fit that evening.

The dinner table never looked more beautiful, dressed in its white linen, a spring bouquet of flowers for a centerpiece. The food looked mouth-watering. Roasted chicken with dressing, creamy mashed potatoes, giblet gravy, and last summer's canned corn made into a light, golden soufflé. There was a mountainous chocolate cake dripping with butter icing for dessert. The cook had surely been given definitive directions to make them all ravenous. Gallio couldn't remember when he'd felt so hungry, while Fred Slager sat in his chair, a linen napkin stuffed into his collar covering his cravat as he rubbed his chubby hands together.

Food was passed, and passed again, around the table until servings of dessert were finished too.

Teresa stood, and as the maid cleared, she told the men to please feel free to go into the parlor for coffee. She followed.

"I understand that you spent some time in Paris these past few months?" Fred questioned Matthew.

"Yes, but it was really a brief business trip." He couldn't bring himself to relate his real mission.

"I've always wanted to travel abroad," Fred continued. "Perhaps before long I'll do just that. But I'd better not wait too much longer." He laughed his hearty guffaw. Teresa was very quiet.

The conversation slowed. Teresa started coughing very softly and looking with knowing eyes at Fred.

Finally realizing her hinting coughs were not noticed by the banker, she spoke. "Matthew, I believe Fred has something to talk with you about. Don't you?" She stared at Slager.

Taking a quick sip of coffee, he straightened up in his chair and faced Matthew. "Yes, yes.... Matthew, I have asked your sister to become my bride...and she has said yes. Now we would like your blessing." He turned almost purple with the effort of announcing their marriage plans. Teresa, too, blushed and looked at her shoes.

These two people whom Matthew had known all of his life intended to wed. He was almost speechless, but not quite. He left his chair and walked over to Teresa. Leaning over her, he kissed her tenderly on the cheek. "My dear sister, you must know by now that all I want for you is your happiness." Then turning to Fred Slager, he extended his right hand. The two men shook hands firmly.

"I want you to know, Matthew, that I don't intend to leave you in the lurch. My intentions are to stay here at the lodge until you have a suitable housekeeper. Fred and I have discussed it thoroughly. We hope to be married by next spring."

"Please, Teresa, don't postpone your plans over the keeping of the house."

"No, we insist. You are to be settled here first. Then Fred walked toward Teresa, putting an arm around her waist.

"I realize this is bound to be a surprise to a lot of people, but it has not been sudden. We have found that we have much in common and we have been meeting and talking for quite some time. Teresa is a very mature young woman with understanding beyond her years. I have grown to love her with all my heart and hope she loves me too." Teresa had tears in her eyes, as she gently patted Fred's hand. "I want to spend what time I have left just trying to show her how much she means to me."

Matthew had a hundred thoughts running through his head...not the least being the question of age difference between the two. But looking at them standing before him, he had to admit that it made no difference, looking at the respect and love they seemed to share.

Matthew spoke sincerely. "My best wishes to you both. This calls for a toast." The wine was brought by the maid and good cheer prevailed.

****

Life went on as usual that summer, with Teresa in charge and Matthew hiking the mountain paths, visiting with his old friends, and sketching ideas for future paintings. Good to his word, he sent a note to Glenn House requesting a visit with Agatha Glenn.

An answer, delivered by Agatha's maid Minnie, arrived soon after his request. A time was set for his visit.

The grandfather clock in the entry hall at Glenn House reminded Matthew of times gone by when he first was commissioned to paint Agatha, then Dolly.

Millie beamed a lovely smile as she led him up the winding staircase to Agatha's rooms. She knocked gently on the door of Mrs. Glenn's sitting room.

Matthew felt that the house seemed empty and abandoned, although it surely was not. Its beautiful appointments gave off an aura of loneliness...too quiet, too untouched. The lovely spicy smells from a busy kitchen, which he recalled, no longer wafted through the house. The word was that Conrad Glenn spent little time at home anymore, traveling on "business trips" to almost anywhere he could think of to keep himself away from the dark karma that seemed to surround his home since Jordan's death.

Millie, getting no answer, tapped lightly again on the oak door. "Come in, Millie; has Matthew arrived?" Agatha's voice, once resonant and strong, quivered. She was sitting in her favorite rocker near the sitting room window, a bible in her lap. Matthew thought she had aged ten years in the brief time since he had last seen her. She remained seated, and as he approached her, she offered her hand, which he held briefly to his lips.

"My, you have become the gentleman. I'm so pleased to see you, Matthew. Please sit down." She motioned him to a chair nearby. He was hatless and his black hair shone. She seemed to inspect him from head to toe. A bit self-conscious in her presence, he ran his fingers through his hair. "It is such a pleasure to see you again, Mrs. Glenn. Teresa speaks of you often; she enjoys the time she spends with you."

"A sweet girl, she is like another daughter to me. A consolation in my time of sorrow. I see Dolly only infrequently...she is busy with her job in Philadelphia."

"I had the pleasure of seeing your daughter at a gathering I attended in Philadelphia. She looked splendid."

"Dolly has more than fulfilled my expectations for her to have a career, but it would be nice if she lived a bit closer to home." Agatha's voice trailed off. Then seeming to straighten herself, she said, "Enough about that. Tell me about yourself."

"There isn't a lot to tell. I have leased a house and studio in Philadelphia where I can be close to the galleries—where I can work during the winter months. It's a quaint old house, well suited to my work."

"Do you intend to desert Queen's Escape?"

"No. It will always be my real home. I plan on being at the lodge about six months of the year."

"That's good! We'd hate to lose you...after all you are our own here." He was touched.

"I did make a trip to New York recently. There is much talk about the building of a grand art museum in the city. Of course that holds my interest." He did not mention Paris.

"That would be a wonderful acquisition for New York and all of us." Agatha seemed to become confused for a moment. Finally she turned sad eyes toward Mathew again. "I was pleased to hear that Goldy Wojna became so successful. Of course her marriage was a surprise, but a pleasant one. I hope she finds much happiness."

"It was a beautiful wedding. She and James Peabody were both close friends of mine. A good match, I believe."

As quickly as their visit had begun, it was obvious that it was over. Agatha seemed to go inside herself, her lips moving soundlessly.

Matthew stood, taking her soft hand in his. May I come again before I leave for the winter season?'

"Whaa—oh, yes yes, of course, Matthew, come again."

Millie showed him out with a troubled look on her face.

"Mrs. ain't good these days."

"I can see that, Millie."

"She broods and cries too much. Sometimes I worry she'll not get well again."

Matthew looked down at the maid who had been with the Glenns so very long. "You are a great help to her...a loving helper in such a bad time." He took his leave.

It did not surprise him that his old friend and patron passed away in her sleep, soon after his visit.

****

The impact of Agatha's death was obvious to all in the town. Her passing was akin to the loss of a well loved relative.

People whose lives had never touched hers were in the funeral procession that flowed toward the local cemetery. She would be long remembered in Franklinton for her generosity, thoughtfulness, civic concerns, and her love of the people.

Dolly, dressed in black from head to toe, sat beside her father, Conrad, in the family carriage that was draped in black.

Each of them sat stiff and unmoving, neither looking at the other for fear the contact of even a look would bring them to collapse.

Matthew and Teresa followed in the second carriage as Teresa wept copiously. "She never deserved such sorrow," Teresa sobbed. "A gentler, sweeter woman never drew breath. The town will sorely miss Mrs. Glenn and all the things she did to help people."

Matthew didn't answer; he just put his arm around his grieving sister, but he was remembering that it was Agatha who gave him his first chance at real portraiture and the success it had started. The portrait, also, of Dolly that made him grow up in a hurry. That time when he first discovered his manhood at Dolly's behest.

His eyes wandered toward the carriage ahead and the woman riding in it—Dolly Glenn, her coil of copper hair covered with a black veil. He wondered if she was thinking of the ashes that were left of her once proud family.

****

The knock on the door at Queen's Escape was answered by Teresa. Surprise lit up her eyes when she saw Dolly standing at the door. "Oh...Miss Glenn, please come in."

"I hope I'm not interrupting you," Dolly questioned.

"Certainly not. Come into the parlor and sit. I was just going to take a break myself and have a cup of tea. Won't you join me?"

"Thank you Teresa. That would be nice."

Teresa hurried to tell the cook to serve tea right away. Then she sat down opposite Dolly in front of the great windows that looked out over the beautiful mountainside.

"This is lovely here; I had no idea..." Dolly spoke softly.

"Yes, it is beautiful and such a shame that Matthew gets to spend so little time here. Why even today when he planned to be here someone insisted on a conference with him about commissioning a historical portrait of someone important in Pittsburgh. He will probably be back tomorrow."

Dolly showed her disappointment that he was not home but continued a friendly conversation with Teresa. "I want to thank you, Teresa, for all of the time you devoted to Mother before her death. She so enjoyed your visits."

The cook brought in the tea tray, and Teresa poured.

"It was a pleasure for me to spend time with her. She was a wonderful friend to me nearly all of my life. I could never repay her for her many kindnesses to me." Conversation lagged.

Dolly gathered up her gloves and reticule, standing to leave. "I must get back, father will be waiting. I'm leaving tomorrow for Philadelphia to return to work. Thank you again for your hospitality, I'm sorry I missed Matthew. Tell him I'm sorry."

Teresa would never know just how sorry, Dolly thought.

Chapter 21: Homeward

ARTHUR COWAN was growing older too. His hair had turned pure white, but his spare frame remained straight. He was as active as ever. His devotion to his art school continued, although he had shortened the winter and summer sessions, finding the slower pace more suitable to him.

The friendship between Matthew and Arthur was still strong—Arthur often referring to Matthew as his "adopted son." He certainly was Matthew's advocate in most things, especially when it concerned Gallio's work. So it was Arthur who brought the news to the young artist that two of his portraits, *The Pink Ribbon* and *Agatha,* had been requested for loan to the New York Gallery for a special exhibit of American portrait artists' work.

"Imagine, Matthew; these were requested by some of the foremost art jurors in the country!"

"But I don't own *Agatha*. How can I give permission when it isn't mine?"

"That should be a small problem. I feel sure Conrad Glenn will be flattered to hear that the gallery wants to show the portrait of his beloved wife.... If you like, I'll have the gallery board's head man contact Conrad Glenn about the loan."

"I think that would be the best approach," Matthew agreed. "How long will they be on loan?" he asked.

"Sometimes an exhibit will run for as much as a year."

"That's a long time. I'm not sure that I want to part with the portrait of Arienne for that long." Matthew walked slowly toward the terrace of Cowan House, remembering a little girl in a mud-streaked dress, holding a bouquet of Arthur's prize geraniums drooping from her small hand.

"You will consider it, won't you, my boy?" Arthur knew how important this opportunity would be for Gallio.

"Yes...I'll consider it." In his heart, he knew he could not disappoint his friend.

The two portraits by Matthew Gallio were received with gratitude and honor by the New York Gallery. The newspapers made note of the Gallio showing as "perhaps, the best American portraiture in the exhibit." *The Pink Ribbon,* the picture of Arienne, was one of the favorites of the show.

Arthur surprised Matthew again a few weeks later when he informed him that he would have to make a trip to Europe. "There is some unfinished business in Paris that I must see to." That was the only explanation Arthur would give to Matthew.

Gallio offered to accompany his friend to Europe. "There's really nothing holding me here right now. Why don't I make the crossing with you?'

Arthur avoided a direct answer, saying, "This is one voyage I must make alone."

Matthew thought it was very odd for his mentor but didn't press him. Arthur Cowan left New York on the sailing ship Antoinette the first day of April, 1876.

In New York, a grand gala was planned as a fundraiser toward the cost of expanding the New York Gallery, to be renamed the Metropolitan Museum of Art.

Everyone from high society had been invited. The prestigious group would meet to view the gallery's gems and drink champagne as they danced the night away. Gallio hated that sort of thing but felt obliged to attend. He would find a corner, he told himself, where he could sit in relative anonymity until he could flee.

****

"Matthew...Matthew Gallio?" He turned around to find himself face to face with Dolly Glenn. She stood before him dressed in a emerald-green chiffon dress that seemed to make her green eyes brighter, her auburn hair radiant. "It seems we are destined to meet at these affairs." Dolly laughed softly. "May I introduce you to Jeffrey Jay? He's a nephew of John Jay. His family is very involved with the Metropolitan Art Museum."

The two men shook hands. Gallio noticed the proprietary air that Jeffrey Jay was showing toward

Dolly. He held her arm firmly, as if he was afraid she would get away.

"Congratulations on the showing of your portraits here. They are very impressive."

"Thank you. It is such a pleasure to me to have your mother's portrait, here." Gallio spoke directly to Dolly.

"Yes, I was very touched when it was chosen, Matthew."

The conversation came to an end. "Please, Dolly, you must come to my studio in Philadelphia when you get back. It would be nice to have you visit me."

"Yes... perhaps."

Jeffrey Jay pulled her gently away.

Gallio stood watching them disappear into the crowd, wondering if he'd ever see Dolly again. He was remembering what might have been.

****

Glad that the hullabaloo was over in New York, Matthew returned to his work in Philadelphia. Nearly three weeks after his return to his studio, he was deep into his work one day when a knock sounded softly on his studio door.

"Matthew...Matthew!" A soft voice called. He quickly opened the door to find Dolly Glenn standing there, looking anxious.

"Dolly! This is a real surprise. Come in...Come in."

He took her hand, leading her to a comfortable chair.

"Forgive me for intruding this way."

"Please, this is a pleasure to have you here." Matthew sat down opposite his old acquaintance. "Will you have some tea or coffee with me? I was about to take a break."

"Thank you, that would be nice—coffee would be good—I've acquired a taste for it since coming to Philadelphia."

The visits from Dolly Glenn to the studio became a weekly occurrence, which Matthew looked forward to. Dolly was good company, with intelligent, sparkling conversation. Not to be overlooked by the artist was her auburn beauty. Her fine figure still held Matthew's attention. It seemed natural, after many weeks, for Gallio to ask Dolly to pose for him again.

"Of course I'll pose for you," she answered in her low, husky voice. "But isn't it about time you were honest with me about it?"

Matthew felt confused by her question. "I have always been honest with you, Dolly."

"The last portrait of me that you painted was less than you wanted...wasn't it?' She walked up close to him, touching his blushing, face. "I'd have done it for you then if you'd have had the courage to ask me." Her lips were soft and warm on his cheek. He took her firmly into his arms, holding her close to him, and covered her mouth with his. It lasted for a long moment as she dug her fingernails into his back. He responded by exploring her neck and the top of her breasts with his tongue.

Pulling away from him, Dolly moved toward a screen that stood in a corner of the room for the models to change behind. She disappeared behind it. Gallio stood transfixed as he watched her clothing being hung, a piece at a time, over the screen. She stepped out from behind the screen totally naked and returned to his side. "Where do you want me to pose?"

Gallio was unsure for a moment about just what to say, then recovering himself, he took her dainty hand in his, leading her to a couch that had a brilliant green satin throw over it. He had her sit on the satin with her right arm up over the back of the couch, her right leg bent, supported against the back of the couch. Her left hand he placed over her auburn mound, with her other leg stretched straight out toward the lower end of the sofa. A large white satin pillow plumped up to support her head. Her white skin looked like porcelain, her green eyes sparkled like emeralds. Her moist lips pouted slightly as if inviting a kiss. This is how he would paint Dolly Glenn.

Dolly's eyes followed his every move as he set up his canvas on the nearby easel. "Please don't move very much," Gallio requested. "It will be uncomfortable after a few minutes, but we'll break for a rest for your muscles at twenty-minute intervals."

She spoke his name softly. "Matthew, please come here." He stopped his preparations to step close to his model. As he leaned over to hear her next words, her soft arms reached up around his neck pulling him to her. "Kiss me again," she ordered him. Unable to resist, he caressed her thigh and breast, much like one would touch a statue by Rodin. Helplessly, he reached for her as if hypnotized. She was so beautiful.

Matthew had had women when he desired, but this woman sent feelings through him he thought he could never feel again. Only Arienne had touched his soul deeper.

For several weeks, Dolly came to pose for Gallio, and offer herself to him. To him, it was a time of pleasure. For her, it was a time of torment, for she knew in her heart that he did not truly love her.

During their last rendezvous, when the painting was done, Dolly told Gallio she would not be back.

"But...but why?" He was mystified.

"I'm going to be married," she told him in a whisper. Tears ran down her cheeks.

"I don't understand..."

"I decided several weeks ago that there was no hope for us...you and me. I've loved you since I was sixteen. But I know you don't really love me...not the way I want you to."

He started to speak...

"Shhhhhhh, my dear, a woman knows when she is truly loved. It's not your fault or mine."

Gallio tried to hold her close. "It's no use, Matthew, it's over. I'm to marry Jeffrey Jay in June."

Matthew stood with his arms slack by his sides. "I'm sorry, Dolly. I do love you, but perhaps you are right...not as much as I should."

"I'm sorry too. Just wish me happiness." Dolly walked out of the studio without looking back.

Chapter 22: The Return

ARTHUR COWAN returned to Philadelphia the end of July. He did not contact Matthew until the first week in August at his mountain lodge. Matthew was unaware that Arthur did not return to the United States alone.

Bartholomew House, closed for several years, had once again come to life. Servants cleaned and polished furniture and floors. The once dead house began to breathe again, its kitchen-heart beat out a daily menu of aromatic foods fit for anyone's taste buds.

In the midst of the house's metamorphosis, a petite young woman, dressed in a plain black dress, drifted from room to room. She touched shining tables, studied family portraits, and gazed into sparkling mirrors, looking at the woman she had become. Her short golden curls shined. Her blue, blue eyes were tinged with wonder. There had been no mirrors at the convent.

Arienne Bartholomew was home after many years. Arthur stayed with her, trying to help her get settled. It was not an easy transition for Arienne. Her health was still fragile.

The sisters of Saint Celeste's Convent had laboriously written a letter to Arthur Cowan early in the spring, telling him that Adrienne (Sister Philipe) had been inconsolable ever since Matthew Gallio's visit. She was no longer flourishing in the environment of the convent...seeming to have no will to live. "Since you are the only close friend she has talked about, we feel bound by God's will to contact you to help us save her life," they wrote to Arthur.

Cowan had answered their plea at once, leaving for France immediately. He found Arienne bedfast, refusing food. "My dear child," he said, bending over her bed, "it's me, Arthur Cowan. Do you remember me?"

The little nun nodded her head.

"Would you like to come back to Philadelphia with me?" Her eyes flew open wide, but she didn't answer; instead, she covered her face with her small hands.

The Mother Superior spent several hours with Arthur discussing Arienne's history and trying to help the artist make a decision about her. "She was very young and frightened when her father, Gerald, brought her to us. He told us he wanted only to have her stay with us until the infant was born. Mr. Bartholomew was very hard on the girl, verbally abusive... condemning her as a sinner for being pregnant without marriage."

Arthur stopped the head nun there. "She was not a wanton girl, she was a good girl who was desperately in love with all of her young heart."

Mother Superior raised one of her hands as if to quiet him. "Arienne believed she had sinned beyond redemption, but I pray that the Lord has long ago forgiven this child. She suffered the wages of sin when her baby was born dead, but then I should not judge."

"Do you think she needs to pay further penance and stay here to, perhaps, die?" Arthur asked.

"That is not our way, Mr. Cowan. We love Sister Philipe, but we think the time has come for her health to be considered first. I am led to believe that she will not survive if she stays in the order. Please, Mr. Cowan, take her back to her home."

"Will she leave the convent?"

"We will explain to her that it has been decreed that she give up the sisterhood because of her health."

During the crossing, Arienne stayed in her cabin most of the time. It was during this journey that Arthur told her of the death of her grandmother and her father. The bitter news caused Arienne to question her right to return to Philadelphia. Each afternoon, Arthur managed to coax her onto the deck for a few minutes, weather permitting. The good food and sea air seemed to make her stronger with each day. "You're getting some color back into your cheeks," he told her.

Her wan smile was payment enough for Cowan. "When we get you home, you'll find your old room waiting for you and the household help anxious to do your bidding. It will be so good to have you back where you belong."

Arienne's eyes failed to show comprehension. "Will I ever belong anywhere again?" She raised her sweet face to him, looking for answers. Arthur smiled down at the gentle girl in the deck chair, wondering to himself if she could ever really go home again. Neither mentioned Matthew Gallio at all.

****

Matthew had traveled back to Queen's Escape for the summer season. Teresa and Fred Slager were winding up their visit to Europe. The wedding had been small, attended only by a few friends.

A cousin of Julia Keep's had settled in nicely as housekeeper for Matthew at the lodge.

Gallio's sense of loss over Dolly Glenn grew less acute with each day. Deep in his heart, he knew such a union would not have lasted.

With the Slagers away and the Glenn house all but vacant except for infrequent visits from Conrad and Dolly, Matthew felt the solitude of the mining town pressing in on him.

Early in October, he wrote to his friend Arthur, asking if he would come to Franklinton for a visit before he left the lodge for the winter season. The answer to his invitation was slow coming. Perhaps, he thought to himself, he should sell the lodge and stay permanently in his home in Philadelphia. He would think about the possibility.

A letter from Arthur posted in the middle of September finally reached Gallio:

Dear Friend;

As you know, I have been back in Philadelphia since the end of July. It has been a challenging period of time for me, and I felt it would be better for all concerned if I kept my reasons for my visit to France a secret.

Now, my dear friend, I am prepared to share with you the trauma that has kept me mute. You must trust me, Matthew, as I reveal the story to you. If you ever kept a level head, it is now time for you to do so again. I know this will shock you as it did me.

Arienne is alive, if barely. She is now living in her old home in Philadelphia. When I found her, she was nearer dead than alive, both physically and mentally depleted. I brought her back to her home to try to have her recover her strength. It will be weeks...perhaps months before she will be herself again. The doctors have every hope for her recovery.

At this point in time, grief is her constant companion since she has learned that both her grandmother and her father are dead. She walks very little except to stroll in the garden, with assistance from her nurse. She looks like a wraith dressed in a black dress, her golden curls still cut very short from the convent. Her speech is minimal except to answer yes or no. You see, old friend, her mental condition is fragile, and it would not be wise for you to come here sweeping her off of her feet.

I will keep you informed about her progress. Please write to me when and if you have questions.

Sincerely,
Arthur Cowan

Matthew sat in his parlor looking at the bare space over the mantel that was awaiting the return of the portrait of Arienne, *The Pink Ribbon*. How could he remain at the lodge knowing that his love was home and alive! But it seemed he had no choice, so he must wait until she was able to acknowledge him. He was confused and sad and, yes, angry—angry at Arthur for keeping the secret so long. Then he thanked God for such a friend as Arthur Cowan.

Thanksgiving was approaching when Matthew finally moved back into his Philadelphia studio. His heart was torn between joy and sadness. The joy of just thinking that Arienne was once more so near, the sadness because he was all but forbidden to go to her.

Arthur met Gallio at a small café near the Bartholomew house. Matthew looked thinner, and worry lines appeared between his eyes. The two friends shook hands and seated themselves at a small table. "When can I see her?" Matthew was very eager.

"I don't know, Matthew. Her recovery seems slow, but she does show some progress."

Matthew clung like a ghost to the neighborhood near her house. His work suffered as well as his health. He wasn't eating properly, and all of Arthur's pleading for him to try to get on with his life was wasted verbiage.

When Christmas was upon them, Arienne seemed to brighten up a bit. She watched the staff put up the Christmas tree, taking some pleasure from the preparations.

After the holidays, her doctors suggested that she try walking a short distance from the house. She didn't know that Matthew sat huddled in a chair at the café, watching through the steamy glass windows for any sign of her.

It was a brilliant, rare sunny day in January when the door at Bartholomew House opened to reveal a starched nurse and a slow-moving Arienne step out onto the stoop. They slowly descended the four steps to the brick sidewalk. Old snow, gray and dirty looking, was melting in the gutters.

The women walked slowly up the sidewalk, picking their way carefully around puddles. Arienne was bundled into a warm fur coat that reached almost to her feet. A matching fur hat shaded her face. As Matthew watched, the two figures moved toward the end of the block.

Hurriedly, Gallio walked across the street from the café to the stoop the two women had just walked down. He stood there waiting for their return, hardly able to breathe. Soon the women approached the house. Arienne kept her head down, stepping slowly. The nurse held her arm firmly.

Matthew stepped in front of the two, his hat in hand, his black hair shining in the sun. "Hello, Arienne. It's so wonderful to see you, again." The women stopped. Arienne raised her face to Matthew's with a startled look, which alarmed the nurse.

"Please, sir, we must get into the house before Miss Bartholomew takes a chill." She gently pulled on Arienne's arm.

As the two former lovers stood looking at each other, Gallio saw Arienne's face flush, then tears streamed down her cheeks, but she did not move. The nurse, not to be ignored, pulled the younger woman through the door, closing it in Matthew's face.

Matthew felt totally shut out of the life of the woman he so desperately loved.

Chapter 23: The Beginning

THE ARTIST left Philadelphia almost immediately after his brief encounter with Arienne; his feelings of hopelessness growing.

It would be the first winter he had stayed in the lodge after Christmas since he inherited the home in the mountains. Emily Titus, his housekeeper, devoted her time to trying to make Gallio comfortable. He spent much of his time working in his studio, painting winter scenes of the mountains, which he had never shown interest in before. The landscapes seemed to soothe his nerves. Memories could intrude without causing him to wrongly shade the color of someone's eyes or the length of a nose. The intense concentration needed for portrait painting was not a factor with his lovely winter scenes.

Emily knocked on his studio door to announce that Teresa was waiting for him in the parlor. "Tell her I'll be right there as soon as I clean my brushes and hands."

Teresa tried to visit her brother each week. She was aware that he was going through a very difficult time in his life. The snowstorms often made the trip up the mountain from the town nearly impossible. It had been three weeks since her last visit. They greeted with a hug.

"Matthew, dear, you look tired. Are you getting enough rest?"

"Now, Teresa, don't fuss over me. I'm doing quite well and Mrs. Titus takes good care of me."

Nevertheless, Teresa was shocked by the gray in her brother's hair and the deep worry lines between his dark eyes. "Fred and I want you to come for dinner next Saturday...can you come?"

Matthew wanted to say no. His sister was forever playing matchmaker...trying to get him interested in her young women friends. "Yes, of course I'll come. What time?"

"Six will be fine. Matthew, I have a favor to ask you."

"Oh-Oh, now what am I in for?"

"Nothing so odd, really. Fred and I will be celebrating our first anniversary before we know it. I'd like to give him a portrait of me. Just a small one... nothing grand."

"My dear sister, nothing would please me more. Consider it on my schedule as of next week."

Teresa breathed a sigh of relief.

The following months passed quickly for Gallio. He was happy when he was painting. Having his sister in the studio with him so often gave him great pleasure. The portrait was almost finished by April. It was a work of love for him. The soft beauty of a mature Teresa had been delicately transferred to the portrait. It showed a lovely, wise-looking matron whose eyes shined with love. She adored it.

****

Spring came to life in the mountains, with the blooming dogwood trees splashed through the budding green fir trees. Evergreens sprouted their new needle tufts on the tips of their boughs.

The lodge settled into the landscape like a perfect piece to a jigsaw puzzle. Its rustic beauty nestled among the beauteous trees and shrubs.

Matthew was lonely. He was considering a voyage to Paris, thinking it was time he spent time studying the masters there. Yet something held him, week after week, at the lodge, procrastinating. He had heard nothing further from Arthur about Arienne. Perhaps, he thought, he was chasing a fantasy.

Teresa's voice called to him from the front door. "Matthew...Matthew are you up there?" He opened the studio door, calling down to her that he'd be right there.

The noontime sun streamed through a stained-glass angel that was set into a window over the staircase. As he descended the stairs, the light almost blinded him.

It was a late spring day...perfect in every way—warm, sunny, promising rebirth.

"Teresa! What are you doing here this time of the day? I'd have thought you'd be cracking the whip at Mrs. Titus, so to speak, making sure she was going to have lunch ready on time." He laughed and so did Teresa.

I had a yearning to take a walk. I thought you'd like to accompany me on such a lovely day." She took his arm and pulled him toward the door.

"All right, all right. I'll come if you promise me you'll stop playing matchmaker every time I turn around."

She crossed her heart with a twinkle in her eyes. "I don't think I'll ever play matchmaker for you again. That is, if you come at once on our walk." Teresa reached up and kissed her brother's cheek warmly.

"What's this all about...another favor?"

"Come on!" She tugged him along.

They walked slowly down the lane toward the creek crossing. A soft wind made the trees dance. Gallio was thinking of his favorite place by the stream, where he and Arienne first met. He glanced in that direction, seeing some movement. A flash of white, perhaps a deer. He slowed his step, not noticing that his sister was hurrying on ahead. There it was again, by his favorite spot near the creek. His feet took him closer as he peered through the trees.

A girl was walking along the bank of the stream. A young woman, the hem of her white dress held up with one hand, as if to avoid getting it muddy. But it was not working. The bottom of her dress was splashed with mud, as were her bare feet. In one hand, she held a tiny bouquet of purple crocuses.

Matthew stopped in his tracks, almost unable to move. The young woman's back was turned away from him. Then his breath caught as he moved closer to her. She turned, looking up at him in surprise. Golden curls lay on her shoulders; her eyes were the bluest of blue. He stopped near enough to her to touch her, but did not...afraid she would disappear.

Arienne smiled up into his softening eyes, saying only "Matthew," as she tenderly raised her hands to his face. The crocuses fell to her feet.

As she caressed his dear face, one tear ran down her cheek.

Feeling his heart thump, Matthew encircled Arienne with his arms, afraid she was not real. He lifted her to his chest, where he kissed away the tear. It was his love.

Teresa was scurrying into the carriage hidden down the lane among the pine trees. The same carriage she had driven Arienne in that brought her back to Matthew. Her tears were of sheer joy as she hurried the horse down the mountain toward her home.

Matthew and Arienne had all but forgotten she was there.

You might also enjoy Alice Louise's engaging short stories:

Short Stories for Long Trips: Journey from Memoir to Fantasy

Are you frustrated by the many unfinished novels that line your shelves or crowd your tablet? You want to make time to read, but you're constantly on the go. If this is you, then it's time to discover, or rediscover, the poignant world of the short story.

Each one of these captivating, adult tales has been artfully crafted to bring you rich characters and memorable passage through a world of familiar places, as well as entrance to places unknown. Expect the unexpected as you travel this road.

Drama, suspense, passion, humor, and the fantastic are all at your fingertips. Take a few minutes to escape to another time, another place. Enjoy the ride.

Short Stories for Long Trips is available at Amazon.com in electronic and paperback versions and through other fine retailers in the electronic version.

Soon to be published: Alice Louise's second anthology, **A Universe of Verses and Stories**.